PENGUIN CRIME FICTION

WAXWORK

Born and educated in England, Peter Lovesey headed
the education department at Hammersmith College
until 1975, when he began writing full time. Over the
past decade his Victorian crime novels have won him a
devoted following in the United States and in England.
His novels include *Wobble to Death, The Detective Wore Silk
Drawers, Abracadaver, Mad Hatter's Holiday, Invitation to a
Dynamite Party, A Case of Spirits,* and *Swing, Swing Together*
(the last three titles are published by Penguin Books). In
addition to his many crime novels, Lovesey has written
extensively on sports and sports history. Peter Lovesey
lives in Middlesex, England, with his wife and their two
teenage children.

WAXWORK

PETER LOVESEY

PENGUIN BOOKS

Penguin Books Ltd, Harmondsworth,
Middlesex, England
Penguin Books, 625 Madison Avenue,
New York, New York 10022, U.S.A.
Penguin Books Australia Ltd, Ringwood,
Victoria, Australia
Penguin Books Canada Limited, 2801 John Street,
Markham, Ontario, Canada L3R 1B4
Penguin Books (N.Z.) Ltd, 182–190 Wairau Road,
Auckland 10, New Zealand

First published in Great Britain by
Macmillan London Limited 1978
First published in the United States of America by
Pantheon Books 1978
Published in Penguin Books 1980
Reprinted 1981

LIBRARY OF CONGRESS CATALOGING IN PUBLICATION DATA
Lovesey, Peter.
Waxwork.
Reprint of the 1978 ed. published by Pantheon Books,
New York.
I. Title.
[PZ4.L89914Wax 1980] [PR6060.O86] 823'.9'14 79-21740
ISBN 0 14 00.4887 1

Printed in the United States of America by
Offset Paperback Mfrs., Inc., Dallas, Pennsylvania
Set in Baskerville

SUNDAY, 15th APRIL

There was nothing shifty about James Berry's eyes. No sideward glance or drooping lids. They were wide and steady. The *Telegraph* had called them codfish eyes once. After that he had changed to the *Graphic*.

The eyes were scanning it now, line by line, column by column. The reports on criminal matters, headed *Police Intelligence*, interested him most. Over the mantelpiece in the front room of his house in Bilton Place, Bradford, were two gilt frames, each filled with eight small photographs of men and women, mounted on best Bristol board. Each was a convicted murderer.

They were a select bunch. They all came in the *carte-de-visite* size, which showed they were not riff-raff. Two were doctors.

This Sunday evening in 1888 his wife was talking about them. 'I believe I could *stand* that lot hanging over my front room mantelpiece if there was summat else up there beside them.'

He looked over his paper. 'What did you have in mind?'

'A picture of you, love.'

It had never occurred to him to put himself up there.

Now that he considered it, he would not look bad in sepia. At thirty-six, he still had most of his hair. His face was manly, right enough, broad and powerful, with a good growth of black beard. There was a deep scar down the right cheek, but the beard covered most of it. He had a notion that his wife liked the scar. She had never inquired how he came by it, but there were times when she traced it with her finger-tips. Ever so lightly.

He told her she was talking rubbish and went back to the *Graphic*. There was a case of poisoning in Kew.

She said the rogues' gallery made her flesh creep. She wanted to look up from her sewing once in a while and see an honest, God-fearing face.

He knew why she mentioned the Almighty. They both took a pride in the lay-preaching. Folk sat up in chapel when James Berry went to the pulpit. He could speak with authority on the wages of sin.

'There's that elegant studio in Bridge Street,' she went on. 'You know – with velvet at window? I've seen what he can do. Beautiful likenesses. You can wear your chapel suit and butterfly collar. You'll make a grand picture, Jim!'

He told her straight that he did not hold with photography. She said it was no sin as far as she was aware. There was nothing about it in the Good Book that she could recollect.

He did not hold with sarcasm either. If it had not been the Sabbath he would have cuffed her for that. He told her so. She went out to make the cocoa.

The *Graphic* had a lot to say about the Kew murder. It seemed they had arrested a young married woman. Her people were well-to-do. They would see she was well represented at the trial. Someone of the calibre of Clarke or Russell was expected to lead the defence. A classic trial was in prospect.

When she appeared with his mug and a biscuit he told her why he had no intention of going to the studio in Bridge Street. 'In my sort of work you don't go out of your way to be recognised. You get enough of that, without photographs. If I had my picture took in Bradford, inside the hour it would be in t' shop window with *James Berry, Public Hangman* in large letters under it.'

She was unimpressed. 'We've no cause to be ashamed, Jim. If folk round here want to see your likeness, why not let them?'

He told her Bradford folk did not matter. They knew him mostly, any road. The trouble would start when some newspaper reporter came by. He would be into that shop like a ferret. Next thing, the picture would be plastered over every paper in the kingdom. It might easily cost them the job.

That silenced her.

No more was said on the matter that evening. Yet Berry did not dismiss it from his mind.

WEDNESDAY, 6th JUNE

The trial of Miriam Cromer took place at the height of the London season of 1888. It was fixed for the week before Ascot, at the Central Criminal Court.

The preliminary hearings at the inquest and police court had set out the facts like visiting cards. The deceased, Josiah Perceval, had been employed as assistant to Mr Howard Cromer, the owner of a photographic studio in Kew. It was a fashionable place, patronised by society. The name of Cromer was familiar to readers of *The Tatler*. On the afternoon of Monday, 12th March, a Dr Matthew Eagle had visited the studio, not to have his photograph taken, but to confirm that Josiah Perceval was a dead man.

The cause of death was poisoning. The post mortem on 14th March confirmed the presence of potassium cyanide, one of the fastest-acting poisons known to science. The dregs of a glass of madeira beside Perceval's corpse had been analysed and found to contain the poison. A bottle of Scheele's solution of potassium cyanide was kept in the processing room at the studio for use as a fixing agent. It was found in the poison cabinet half empty.

The first theory of the police was suicide. Perceval had been found alone. No one else had been in the studio rooms for two hours. He was understood to have had financial worries. He owed his bookmaker sixty-seven pounds.

The suicide theory was discarded when a decanter of madeira found in a chiffonier in the

8

studio was analysed and found to contain cyanide. A man proposing to poison himself would put the poison in the glass he drank from, not the decanter. The person in the house responsible for keeping the decanters topped up was the proprietor's wife, Mrs Miriam Cromer. She had attended to it at noon on the day of Perceval's death. Before two o'clock she had gone out to her dressmaker's for a fitting. Her husband was in Brighton for a meeting of the Portrait Photographers' League, so Perceval was alone in the studio. It was an open secret that he helped himself to madeira when he had the opportunity.

At twenty minutes past three the housekeeper and a maidservant who were in the basement underneath the studio heard a heavy thump as if someone had fallen. It was followed by other sounds, a series of knocks as if someone were beating upon the floor. There was an order that no servant was to be seen in the studio in business hours, but the sounds were so unusual and alarming that they took it upon themselves to investigate. They found Perceval lying rigid on the carpet, fighting for breath, his eyes glassy and staring, his skin turning blue. He was conscious but incapable of speech.

The maid ran to fetch Dr Eagle, but in the ten minutes it took for him to be summoned, Perceval died.

Mrs Miriam Cromer returned to the house shortly before four o'clock. She came directly to the studio. Asked whether she knew if there was any form of poison in the house, she took

9

Dr Eagle to the cabinet and showed him where the cyanide was kept. A few minutes later she fainted.

During the next week painstaking work by the police discovered a remarkable collation between the financial affairs of Josiah Perceval and certain transactions made by Miriam Cromer. In October and December, 1887, and January and February, 1888, Perceval had settled debts with his bookmaker of £10, £12, £14 and £15 respectively. At dates that closely corresponded, Mrs Cromer had visited a Brentford pawnbroker and obtained precisely similar sums. On the advice of her solicitor, Mr Simon Allingham, she declined to appear as a witness at the inquest on 28th March. The coroner's jury returned a verdict of wilful murder against her. That same afternoon she was formally charged and taken into custody.

At the magisterial hearing on 9th and 10th April, Allingham appeared for Miriam Cromer. When the charge was put he instructed her not to speak, and then reserved her defence. She was committed for trial at the Old Bailey.

In the next two months, public interest reached such a pitch of intensity that the sheriffs decided to issue special admission tickets to the public gallery of Number One Court. At Eton's Fourth of June celebration these were changing hands for ten guineas. By Derby Day on the sixth, the price had risen to fifteen. It was rare to see a beautiful woman brought to justice accused of causing a man's agonising death; positively not to be missed when there were possibilities of salacious overtones. Such cases passed into legend. No sixpenny novel ever published rivalled the candour of the disclosures in court of Miss Madeleine Smith's indiscretions with her French lover, Florence Bravo's adultery with an ageing doctor, or Adelaide Bartlett's intimacy with a minister of the Wesleyan Church. In the case of Miriam Cromer no-one needed telling that the payments to Josiah Perceval suggested blackmail. The nation caught its breath and prepared for revelations.

They came in a way nobody expected. A week before the start of the trial Miriam Cromer made a confession. It was drawn up as an affidavit and she was taken from her remand cell in Newgate Prison to put it on oath before a magistrate.

The first the public heard of it was on 6th June, two days before the trial. An occasion that should have been a legal formality, the charge of the Bill of Indictment before the Grand Jury, was galvanised when Mr Justice Colbeck began to read:

'I, Miriam Jane Cromer, wife of Howard Cromer, wish voluntarily to state that on the afternoon of Monday, 12th March, 1888, at Park Lodge, Kew Green, I murdered one Josiah Perceval, photographic assistant in my husband's employment. I added potassium cyanide to a decanter of wine knowing that he was likely to drink from it and be fatally poisoned. My reason for committing this act was that for a period of several months Josiah Perceval had subjected me to blackmail.

'In the summer of 1882, when I was twenty years of age and lived at my family home in Hampstead, I injudiciously agreed to take part with two friends in some photographic sittings based on themes of classical antiquity. We were members of the Highgate Literary and Artistic Society and we had been advised that the photographs were to be used as preliminary studies for a painting by Sir Frederick Leighton, now Lord Leighton, the President of the Royal Academy. This was not the case. However, at the time and for some years after, we believed it to be so. Some half-dozen photographs were taken and for certain of them we were unclothed, or draped in diaphanous muslin. I can only account for our *naïveté* by stating that the lady, now deceased, who effected the arrangements was a leading member of the Society and a distinguished resident of Highgate.

'In September, 1885, I was married and left Hampstead to live in Kew. My husband, Mr Howard Cromer, was the proprietor of a reputable photography studio at Park Lodge, Kew Green. In his employment was Mr Josiah Perceval, who had been engaged as studio assistant a few months before I came to Park Lodge. I cannot say that I knew Mr Perceval well, because my husband preferred me not to assist with the business, except in emergencies. I would sometimes attend to the reception of clients and I also arranged the flowers in the studio and kept the decanters filled.

'One morning in October, 1887, I had

brought some chrysanthemums into the studio when Mr Perceval, who happened to be alone there, surprised me by stating that he had a matter of business to discuss with me. To my shame and distress he thereupon produced a photograph which I recognised as one taken in Hampstead five years before, said to depict the Three Graces. One of the unclad figures was unmistakably myself. In a manner calculated to aggravate my humiliation, Mr Perceval informed me that he had purchased it at a shop in Holywell Street, off the Strand, which purveyed photographs of a similar character, and worse. He then offered to sell me the picture for the sum of ten pounds. When I protested, he said that if I preferred, he would do business with my husband, and if *he* were not interested, there were people in Kew who were likely to be.

'When I had recovered sufficiently from the mortification of what had been suggested, I considered my position and realised that I must yield to his infamous demand. Even if I faced the humiliation of informing my husband of the business, it would serve no practical purpose. Howard would be obliged to dismiss the man from his employment. There were certain to be recriminations. Mr Perceval would see that the matter became the gossip of every drawing-room in Kew. The fragile reputation of our business, so laboriously built, would be shattered overnight.

'At the next opportunity I secretly visited a pawnbroker's in Brentford and obtained ten pounds, in exchange for which I pledged some items of jewellery. When my husband went out of the house the day after, I paid the sum to Mr Perceval. Not content with the money he had extorted, he proceeded to make a number of offensive remarks about the photograph, influenced, I was sure, by a substantial intake of my husband's madeira wine which he unashamedly drank in my presence. When at last he handed me the photograph I burned it forthwith.

'The possibility that he had other photographs in his possession had not escaped me, but I dared not inquire, because he might otherwise have been unaware of their existence. My fears were confirmed a month later when he told me that his bookmaker was becoming troublesome about a debt of twelve pounds and he was prepared to sell me a print entitled *Aphrodite With Handmaidens* for the same.

'In all, I made four payments between October, 1887, and February, 1888. The sums involved were not large, but it was necessary for me to visit the pawnbroker each time, since I had no means of obtaining money other than the few shillings I had from my husband for small personal needs. Over the months, Mr Perceval's manner towards me became increasingly unendurable. However, I clung to the knowledge that his supply of the photographs could not be limitless – vainly, as it transpired. In March he informed me that he had made inquiries in Holywell

Street as to the source of the photographs and learned that they were taken in Hampstead. He intended purchasing the original plates from which they were printed. His expenses, he said, were likely to be considerably higher than he could afford from the salary my husband paid him, so it would be necessary for me to advance him the sum. He expected it to be of the order of a hundred and fifty pounds.

'My agony was complete. I was expected to supply an amount of money quite beyond my resources to provide my blackmailer with the means to persecute me for as long as he cared. For a week I struggled with the problem, trying to devise some way of resolving it. To capitulate to the demands, I now realised, would only postpone the day when I would have to act. To confide in my husband was no solution; it would only extend the blackmail to Howard, who could not risk a scandal any more than I. The studio was now patronised by distinguished clients, people of high standing in the community who would be outraged by the knowledge that their photographer's wife had so far debased herself as to pose for pictures of that type. Our very livelihood was in Mr Perceval's hands. The only release I could envisage was that Providence might put an end to his life, a possibility too remote to contemplate. Yet as the hours passed and I struggled in my anguish to find some way of extricating myself from my predicament, my tortured thoughts turned repeatedly to that eventuality. It occurred to me that I had the means to expedite it.

'There was a bottle of potassium cyanide in the studio. It was one of the chemicals occasionally used in the developing process. My husband was extremely conscious of its dangerous properties, frequently warning me that it was a deadly poison and was on no account to be removed from the poison cabinet except by himself. In my desperation to end my torment I devised a plan to administer potassium cyanide to Mr Perceval in such a way that his death would be taken for suicide.

'I have mentioned that I was accustomed to attend to the decanters which my husband keeps in the studio in order to offer a glass of wine to his sitters. The weekly order of wine is sent from Morgan's in Brentford and arrives by noon on Mondays. At lunch-time I fill the decanters with fresh sherry, port and madeira.

'On Monday, 12th March, my husband had engaged to attend a convention of the Portrait Photographers' League, of which he is Vice-Chairman, in Brighton, where he was to stay overnight, returning Tuesday morning. We had no sittings arranged for that day, so I knew that Mr Perceval would be working alone in the studio, developing the previous week's dry plates. I also knew that he was likely to help himself liberally to my husband's madeira. In the morning I waited as usual for the wine to arrive and then took the bottles to the studio and filled the decanters.

'When Mr Perceval went out for lunch at one o'clock, I returned to the studio, unlocked the poison cabinet, found the bottle of potassium cyanide and poured about a third of the contents into the decanter of madeira. I then replaced the decanter in the chiffonier where it was kept with the others, and locked the cyanide bottle in the poison cabinet as before.

'Soon after, I went out to keep an appointment at my dressmaker's in Sandycombe Road, confident of finding Mr Perceval dead when I returned. The action of cyanide, my husband had often impressed on me, was practically instantaneous and quite fatal. I had convinced myself there was no chance of the body being discovered prematurely, as the servants were under strict orders not to enter the studio rooms in business hours. I intended on my return to arrange things to give the appearance of suicide, placing the bottle of cyanide beside the wine glass from which he had drunk, and emptying the decanter of its poisoned contents, re-filling it with fresh madeira. After searching the pockets of his suit for photographs or documents that might incriminate me, I would call the servants and raise the alarm.

'I duly returned a few minutes before four o'clock to learn that my plan had gone irretrievably wrong. The body had been discovered and Dr Eagle had already examined it. My understanding of the effects of potassium cyanide had been in error. Mr Perceval had not died instantaneously. His convulsions had been so frantic and so prolonged that two of the servants had seen fit to disregard their orders and rush to the studio to investigate. They had found him dying, unable to speak. The housemaid, I was told, had gone to fetch the doctor, who had recognised the symptoms of cyanide poisoning.

'There was nothing I could do to alter the eventual conclusion that Mr Perceval had been murdered, although Dr Eagle made no statement on the matter to me, simply asking where the poison was kept. I unlocked the cabinet and showed him the bottle of potassium cyanide. He sent one of the servants for the police and another for Mr Allingham, the family solicitor. Soon after this I was seized with the gravity of my situation, and fainted. When I had recovered sufficiently for the police inspector to question me, I pretended to have no knowledge of the events leading to Mr Perceval's death.

'I swear that this is a true statement superseding all other statements ascribed to me and signed by my hand this first day of June, 1888.
Miriam Jane Cromer'

Mr Justice Colbeck cautioned the Grand Jury that the law does not regard a confession in itself as establishing incontrovertible evidence of guilt, but that independent evidence taken in association with the statement warranted him to advise them that it was their duty to find a True Bill against Mrs Cromer.

The True Bill was returned.

FRIDAY, 8th JUNE

The trial itself opened on a morning of over-
cast sky and heavy rain. The chandeliers were
turned up in Number One Court at 10 a.m.
The ushers opened the doors of the public
gallery and it filled in little more than a minute,
the jewellery in the gaslight confirming that it
was still a fashionable occasion, even if the
confession had removed the uncertainty over
the outcome.

The call to rise came at 10.35 a.m. Mr Justice
Colbeck was wearing the ermine-trimmed scarlet
robe of the Queen's Bench Division. He carried
a pair of white gloves in his left hand and a
piece of black material in his right. Without
looking up, he deposited them on the bench
beside the small posy of flowers to his right.
Then he drew his robe forward and took his
seat under the sword of justice. The court
settled again.

The prisoner was called to the bar.

All week the illustrated newspapers had
supplied their readers with artists' 'impressions'
of Miriam Cromer. They were strikingly at one
with each other. And with the faces of the
young women advertising Pear's, Cadbury's and
Eno's.

People craned for a view of the woman as she
was. Flanked by two wardresses, she mounted
the steps from the passage under the dock a
few minutes before the judge's procession entered. Those seated nearest had heard the click
of the dock-handle, but the prisoner had been

kept well back, obscured in a group that included the keeper of Newgate Prison, the chaplain and a doctor. Now the wardresses steered her to the front.

She faced the judge without gripping the rail, a slight figure in that vast dock.

She was wearing black, as was customary. Her clothes were fashionable, even so: a zouave jacket in velvet over an Ottoman silk gown with jockey sleeves and jet fastenings. The line of the skirt was augmented dramatically by a crinolette, a bustle worn low in the latest style. She was not veiled. The crownless velvet toque high on her head accented the honey colour of her hair in the artificial light. It was styled of necessity in a simple fashion, drawn back severely to a chignon.

Her features, profiled against the dark panelling, betrayed no anguish. Rather she seemed to repudiate sympathy in the way she held her head so that her throat and jaw formed an angle as sharp as the outline of the dock. Her lips curved naturally in a shape that could have been taken for the start of a smile if it were not corrected by the slight contraction of muscles in her cheek, dignifying the expression. Her skin was smooth and very pale. She had a fine nose, delicate, arched eyebrows and a high, intelligent brow. What ambushed the expectations of the packed court were the eyes of the accused woman – eyes, the least susceptible of all the features to the pens of newspaper illustrators. Hers held no shame. Almost violet in their blueness and dark-edged from weeks in prison cells, those eyes were unforgettable. Dignified, resolute and steady.

So steady.

There was an air of suspended animation about her, giving her the look of a figure in wax.

The indictment was read: 'Miriam Jane Cromer, you stand charged with having at Kew in the County of Surrey on the twelfth of March, 1888, wilfully and with malice afore-thought, killed and murdered one Josiah Perceval. How say you: are you Guilty or Not Guilty?'

She answered clearly and without hesitation, 'Guilty.'

At the request of the judge, the Attorney-General, representing the Crown, made a statement summarising the facts of the case, showing how the evidence substantiated the confession of the accused.

Counsel for the Defence, Mr Michael Gaskell, Q.C., then rose to say, 'My lord, the prisoner wishes to inform the court that she alone is guilty of this crime. In affirming her readiness to atone for her guilt, she asks that consideration be given in judgment to the painful and insupportable circumstances that induced her to perpetrate the crime.'

Mr Justice Colbeck tersely answered, 'The prerogative of mercy does not rest with me. The plea must be recorded.'

The Clerk of the Court faced the dock. 'Miriam Jane Cromer, you have confessed your-self guilty of the wilful murder of Josiah Perceval. Have you anything to say why the court should not pronounce sentence upon you?'

Her left hand moved towards the rail. The rings on the third finger glittered in the light.

'You must answer,' said the judge.

'I have nothing to say, my lord.'

The oblong of cloth known as the black cap was placed on the judge's head.

'Prisoner at the bar, you have been convicted on your own admission of the dreadful crime laid to your charge. I have studied the evidence and examined the deposition you made concerning your actions and I can entertain no doubt as to your guilt. That the deceased by your account behaved shamefully and criminally towards you I concede, but whether that may be weighed in mitigation is not for me to say. There were other remedies open to you than murder, which is the most heinous of all crimes. I am bound to say that yours was an odious form of murder. The use of poison necessarily involves an element of calculation. This was not an impulsive act; it was a crime deliberately planned. You carried it out in cold blood.

'As I have already made clear to you, the law leaves me no discretion, and I must pass on to you the sentence of the law; and it is that this court doth ordain you to be taken hence to the place from whence you came, and from thence to the place of execution, and that you be there hanged by the neck until you are dead; and that your body be afterwards buried within the precincts of the prison in which you shall have been confined after your conviction, and may the Lord have mercy on your soul.'

The eyes of everyone were on the small figure in the dock. The sentence had not disturbed her waxlike stillness. A wardress touched her arm to indicate that she must turn and go down the steps. She inclined her head, turning to her right, away from the judge. For a moment her eyes appeared to linger on someone in the well of the court. Then she allowed the wardresses to lead her down and out of sight.

That ritual over, another began. On the steps down from the dock the wardresses gripped the prisoner firmly by each arm. In the brown-tiled passage underneath they held her upright while the doctor administered sal volatile. Whether it was required was not considered. They took her into a room and sat her on a bench. The doctor offered brandy, but she shook her head. She appeared to be in control. The doctor took her wrist and felt the pulse.

The chaplain who had waited unobtrusively came forward, opening his Bible.

Miriam Cromer turned to one of the wardresses and asked, 'When will you be taking me back to the prison?'

'When you are fit to walk.'

'I can walk now.' Before the chaplain could begin his spiritual comfort she told him, 'I am not ungrateful, but at this moment I want to be taken wherever I must and then left alone.'

The doctor nodded his assent. The wardresses,

both strong women, took hold of her arms and practically lifted her from the bench.

The Central Criminal Court was linked with Newgate by a stone passage open to the elements. It was commonly known as Birdcage Walk, from the iron bars in default of a roof. The rain was teeming in.

They hustled her forward, heads bowed. After a few steps she hesitated, her attention caught. At intervals capital letters had been crudely chiselled in the flagstones. Isolated letters. 'Better you don't ask,' one of the wardresses told her firmly. 'Take a squint at the sky. You won't see much of it where you're going.'

There was a stone porch at the end. They stood there breathing rapidly from the quick walk through the rain while a turnkey opened the iron-plated door to the prison.

Newgate had undergone extensive alterations thirty years before, but the essential structure was still the four-foot masonry of 1782. The granite blocks stood as they had for a century, undisguised by tiles or plaster, grey at the entrance, lime-washed in the passages ahead.

She was taken into a stone-floored room on the right and brought before a blue-uniformed man at a desk. For more than a minute the group of three women waited in silence while he finished writing something. Then he looked up and confirmed her name and sentence with the wardress on the left.

He addressed the prisoner: 'Christian names?'

'Miriam Jane.'

'*Sir*,' one of the wardresses prompted her.

'Sir.'

'Address?'

She paused, frowned faintly, and gave it.

'Date and place of birth?'

'23rd March, 1862. Hampstead. Sir.'

'Next of kin?'

'That would be my husband Howard.'

'His full name?'

'Mr Howard Cromer, sir.'

'His address?'

'The same as mine.'

'Religion?'

'His, or mine, sir?'

The officer looked up from his writing to decide whether sarcasm was intended.

'Church of England, sir.'

He ordered her to hand over any personal possessions.

She gave him her reticule, locket and engagement ring. She was allowed to keep her wedding ring.

He pushed a paper towards her and told her to sign it. With a firm hand, she wrote her name in full.

Another key was turned and she was taken further into Newgate. Each time a door slammed, the sound reverberated through the building, conjuring an impression of numberless catacombs.

They mounted an iron staircase to the women's wing. Nothing about it was suggestive of femininity. The walls were as solid as the rest of Newgate. A door lined with sheet-iron led into a stone-flagged passage. At the end was a door marked *Lady Superintendent*. They knocked and ushered the prisoner in.

'Come forward, Cromer, and stand where I can speak to you without raising my voice. I am Miss Stones, and I shall be responsible for you while you are here.' Miss Stones spoke with the stiff but not unfriendly manner of a schoolmistress. She was a small, birdlike woman in her fifties, dressed in a grey uniform. Her bonnet was made of better stuff than the wardresses wore. 'There is little that I need to say to you now. We shall get you to your cell as soon as we are able. The regulations stipulate that you must be attended by two prison officers day and night and visited each day by the governor, the chaplain and me. You may also receive visits from your family and your legal advisers. You are permitted to exercise at times when the other prisoners are in their cells and you may attend Morning Service in the Chapel on Sunday. You will address the officers as "miss" and me as "madam". Is that fully understood?'

'Yes, madam.'

Having recited her set piece, Miss Stones took a lace handkerchief from her sleeve and opened it sufficiently for an aroma of cheap scent to declare its presence. In a refined accent she said, 'I am not unaware of the sensibilities of a woman of your position subjected to prison discipline. The regulations, of course, must be obeyed at all times, but there is no reason for you to suffer excessively. If you require something to induce sleep it can be provided.'

'Thank you, madam.' The prisoner answered as mechanically as Miss Stones had begun. Her eyes were empty of any emotion.

The prison staff recognised her manner as indicative of a state of shock they had met before in prisoners straight from sentencing. Quite soon she was likely to be weeping, possibly to the point of hysteria.

Miss Stones nodded to the wardresses. They took the prisoner out and into a passage lined with cell doors.

'My name is Bell,' one of them said. She was solid like the walls, and had a pugnacious cast of face, but the voice softened the impression. Before that morning Bell had been prepared to dislike the prisoner as one of the genteel class who thought of themselves as ladies and would no doubt expect to be treated as such, in spite of having savagely murdered a fellow-creature. Yet the manner in which she had stood in the dock and looked that judge in the eye as she had received her sentence and the way she had conducted herself since spoke something for her courage, Bell admitted. 'You'll be seeing plenty of us – Hawkins and me. We do an eight-hour turn, you see, then another pair take over. Six to two this week – that's the easy turn.' She continued talking about the prison routine without interruption from Hawkins, a wiry, thin-faced woman who looked underfed.

At the end of the passage they passed into a large room with a concrete floor. 'Pick yourself a tub,' Bell amiably said, 'and get it filled with water.'

There were four tin baths hanging on hooks from the wall. Below each was a water-tap. With difficulty, because she was slightly built, the prisoner Cromer lifted one down, stood it under the tap and started the water running. Over the drumming, Bell shouted, 'Look alive, then. Take off your things.' She pointed to a row of cubicles facing the taps. They were open-fronted.

The wardresses stood together, waiting. It was not just a challenge to modesty. Miriam Cromer belonged to a class that differentiated itself from people like them by its pretensions to refinement. Undressing was a private activity for her kind.

She looked on the point of speaking. Her eyes met Bell's. She turned, walked to a cubicle, removed her hat and began unfastening her velvet jacket. With that, the wardresses moved to other tasks, Hawkins opening a cupboard to select prison clothes while Bell added disinfectant to the water. 'Buck up, won't you?' she said. 'There'll be the devil and all to pay if Miss Stones comes here and you ain't scrubbed. For a moment just then I thought you was shy of showing your skin. I'll warrant you've got nothing we haven't seen before. Bless you, on Friday nights we have four baths on the go and eight more, naked as cuckoos, waiting. No need to be alarmed. It won't happen to you. It all comes exclusive for your class of prisoner.'

Miriam Cromer finished unlacing and stepped out of her undergarments, frail, girlish in form and difficult to think of as a monster. Goose-flesh was forming on her limbs.

Bell gestured to her to get into the bath.

She obeyed and lowered herself quickly.

'All over, top to tail,' Bell instructed, handing her a bar of yellow soap. 'Hair and all. I should have told you to unpin it first. I'll do it for you.'

'No,' she said quickly. 'I can manage.'

It was spoken as a reflex, without regard to the consequence. Had Miriam Cromer known more about prison she would have realised how rare it was for a wardress to volunteer assistance. This small assertion of independence deprived her of Bell's sympathy from that moment on.

Acidly, the wardress said, 'Please yourself. It doesn't do nothing for me, you know, touching prisoners' hair.'

Hawkins collected the prisoner's clothes and put them one by one into a basket, examining them as if they were in a gown-shop. The chemise and drawers, pretty silk things in pale lemon trimmed with lace, she tossed aside. 'Can't put them away,' she said. 'They'll need washing.'

When the prisoner had rinsed the soap and disinfectant from her hair as far as it was possible under the tap, she put her hands on the rim of the bath and looked to right and left. There was no towel.

Bell stood with arms folded, tacitly challenging her to ask for one to be fetched. Hawkins was still busy with the basket.

After a moment's thought the prisoner stood upright and stepped out of the bath on to the concrete, watched by Bell. She stooped and dragged the bath to a drain in the centre of the floor and tipped away the water. She replaced the bath on its hook. Then she stood, panting from the effort, facing the wardress, her hands hanging loose at her side, resisting the impulse to modesty. The breathlessness turned to shivering, but she said not a word, simply looked at Bell as she had looked at the judge, without shame or fear in her eyes.

Bell spoke first, conceding a small victory to the prisoner. 'There you are, then. No different in your skin from the rest of us. Better get yourself dry. Don't want to catch your death – ' She stopped in mid-sentence, smiled to herself, opened a cupboard and pulled out a towel. It was coarse and far from clean. The prisoner took it and used it.

Hawkins gave her a grey cotton garment, a sort of wrap-over dressing gown, and told her to sit in the cubicle. 'You have to be seen by the doctor,' she explained. 'Weighed, measured, all those things. Regulations. When that's done, we'll get you some prison clothes.'

'What will happen to my own things?'

'*Miss*,' Bell said with a glare. 'If you want to speak to an officer, Cromer, address her in the proper fashion.'

'I'm sorry. I forgot.' A flat statement, neither repentant nor defiant. 'Will they be returned to my husband, miss?'

'No. They must be kept here. You'll be permitted to wear them again' – Bell paused – 'at the end.'

A moment's silence.

'I see. And after that?'

'You don't have to worry, do you?'

'I should like to know if they are returned to my husband, miss.'

In a hard, tight voice, Bell said, 'I can tell you that they are not. Regulations. But if you suppose they come to any of us, you are wrong. For your peace of mind, I suggest you inquire no further, Cromer.'

Detective Sergeant Cribb stood in his sitting-room facing the clock, flexing the muscles of his legs. He was due for a visit from Chief Inspector Jowett. It was not by invitation. The *Police Code* stipulated '*An Inspector is to visit, at least once a month, the lodgings of all sergeants and constables who do not live in Section Houses, to ascertain that the places are fit to reside in, and that there is not any circumstance which makes it improper for the sergeant or constable to live in the house.*' Jack Ottway, the local Inspector for M Division, usually came, drank two cups of tea, and left without moving out of the scullery.

This time, unaccountably, it was to be Jowett. Cribb had received the news an hour ago in a curt memorandum that arrived at Divisional Headquarters in Blackman Street by the last despatch cart from the Yard. Mystified, he had come home to prepare. Jowett was a big pot now, a Chief Inspector, on three hundred a year. He should have more important things to do than grubbing round men's homes.

Ten years before, when they had served together at Stoke Newington, Jowett had been a regular infliction. He would comb the place for signs of damp and vermin while Cribb looked on, red-eyed with resentment. Really nothing personal was intended. Jowett simply treated the *Code* as an article of faith. By championing it he expected to be chosen for higher things. It had not failed him. He had gone from Second Class Inspector to First Class within a year.

They had given him an office of his own at the
Yard. And a telephone-set. Now he was one of
only three Chief Inspectors in the C.I.D. While
Cribb remained a sergeant.

The *Code* told him why. '*Any officer who
wishes for early advancement has frequent
opportunities of attracting the notice of his
superiors by some action evidencing zeal, ability
and judgment, by strict attention to duty,
sobriety and a smart appearance, and respectful
demeanour.*' Cribb's conduct satisfied each condition but the last. His demeanour was not
respectful. Too often he had made it plain that
he could not abide Jowett. That impediment to
promotion should have been removed when
Jowett took up his position at the Yard, but
Jowett would not let him alone. Now, not content with calling him to the Yard each time a
problem landed on his desk, he was coming out
to Bermondsey to persecute him in his home.

A movement caught his eye. Only the cat,
standing up to stretch. He envied its repose.
Cribb's was a restless temperament. It showed
in his physique. Fifty now, his hair more grey
than black, he was as lean as he had been on the
parade-ground at Canterbury in his army days.
And practically as fit. He had been stopped a
shilling for a day's sickness perhaps a dozen
times in his career, no more. Occasionally he
begrudged the Yard his diligence, yet he could
no more change it than his nose, which was
worthy of an Indian chief. Sharp, too, in speech,
quick to spot deceit, his sense of irony kept him

tolerant of others in most situations. He often fumed, rarely erupted.

He eyed the cat circumspectly. Just his luck if it had brought in a flea. He bent closer.

The sound of carriage wheels outside brought him upright. By looking into the mirror at an angle he watched the hansom draw up outside. Jowett, without a doubt. George Road, Bermondsey, was not a cab-hiring neighbourhood.

'Jerusalem!'

Jowett had stepped out of the cab. He was wearing a top hat and frock coat.

Cribb went downstairs in case the docker under him should answer the door.

Jowett stepped inside without a word, handing Cribb the hat and kid gloves as he passed.

'Upstairs,' murmured Cribb.

Jowett took them two at a time. A rake of a man, he moved with an impression of agility. It was physical only.

'In here?'

'Wherever you care to start,' Cribb was in braces and a collarless shirt: no dressing up for this.

'Is, er, Mrs Cribb . . . ?'

'Out.' He had sent Millie to visit her sister in Rotherhithe. She still believed the Yard would make him up to inspector if he treated Jowett right. On an inspector's wage they could visit the theatre sometimes. Millie's idea of Heaven was the dress circle at Drury Lane. She could tell you what was running at every theatre in London. If she had known Jowett was coming, she would have put out the best teacups and made some cakes as well.

'Good.'

'Eh?'

'Don't misunderstand me,' said Jowett quickly. 'Better I should see you alone.'

'I thought it was the house you had come to see.'

'That was the impression I wanted to give. The facts are otherwise.'

They were facing each other at the top of the stairs.

'If you haven't come to inspect my living arrangements . . .'

'Cribb, we've known each other a long time.'

'Twelve years. That doesn't mean I'm obliged to – '

'Let's dispense with formalities, shall we?'

Cribb turned the silk hat thoughtfully in his hands. 'I generally do in my own house.'

'Is there, by any chance' – Jowett's eyes darted about – 'anywhere suitable for a confidential chat?'

Cribb was about to say there was nothing wrong with the landing when Millie's parting words came back to him. '*Treat him civilly for my sake, love. If he was one of the criminal class you wouldn't think twice about buttering him up to smooth the way, now would you?*' He pushed open the sitting-room door. The cat bolted between them and down the stairs. 'Bit of a change from Whitehall.'

'Ah.' Jowett flicked up the ends of the coat and sat in Cribb's armchair. 'Not much escapes you, Sergeant. I say, you wouldn't object to my pipe?'

Cribb was lost for words. The spectacle of Chief Inspector Jowett installed in his own sitting-room tamping that infernal pipe was more than he could stomach.

'You're absolutely right, of course,' Jowett went on. 'I was at the Home Office this morning. Deuced uncomfortable chairs. Nothing like this.' He brushed some stray shreds of tobacco off his coat. 'Won't you sit down? Dammit, let's forget about rank. It isn't so long since we messed together at Upper Street. That was a time, Cribb. Real detective work.'

Cribb said nothing. In his recollection Jowett's detective work had consisted of writing voluminous reports to Scotland Yard. His career was a testimony to the power of the pen.

'Seems like yesterday,' Jowett reminisced. 'Tell me now, would you by any chance recall a constable named Waterlow? Tall chap. Your sort of build, but losing his hair.'

Waterlow. Cribb remembered. One of Jowett's kind, forever volunteering to write the Morning Report in lieu of beat duty. 'Yes, sir. I heard he was made up to sergeant soon after I left.'

'Inspector now. You knew him tolerably well?'

This required caution. 'No better than you, sir. He was one of the bunch at Islington.' Cribb moved Millie's linnet out of range of the pipe fumes.

'I must say, I rated him a smart young fellow,'

Jowett went on. 'A career man, eager to put up a show.'

'That was my impression.'

'Funny, how wrong you can be about a man,' mused Jowett, staring into the bowl of his pipe. It had gone out. 'Ten years ago, I would have tipped him for a chief inspector's job.'

'Inspector isn't anything to be ashamed of,' said Cribb, keeping himself in check.

'Hm.' Jowett lowered his voice. 'Strictly between these walls, Waterlow is somewhat of a disappointment as an inspector. They didn't think much of him at Bow Street. Made an ass of himself, I'm afraid. He was transferred to V Division. Inspector-in-charge at Kew. A quiet station. It's a large patch, but most of it is the Botanic Gardens. There isn't a lot of serious crime. Or wasn't, until March of this year.' Jowett paused and looked inquiringly across the room.

Like everyone else, Cribb had followed the Kew Poisoning Case. He stood at the window staring down at Jowett's cab. 'Did Waterlow have a hand in that business? I missed his name in the papers.'

'I'm not surprised. It didn't feature very prominently. He was not called at the trial last week because the woman confessed and pleaded guilty.'

'Convenient for V Division, sir. Another case closed.'

'So it would seem.' Jowett's eyes narrowed as he took another match to the pipe. 'Miriam Cromer is now in Newgate under sentence of death. There is, however, a complication. It may be of no consequence at all, but as it was explained to me this morning by' – he paused, busy with the pipe – 'the Home Secretary' – a flame leapt several inches above the bowl – 'it sounded difficult to account for, Sergeant. Now for God's sake will you sit down?'

Cribb let himself slowly into Millie's armchair, not liking the drift of this in the least.

'You will know if you studied the newspaper reports that Mrs Cromer claimed in her confession that she was being blackmailed by the victim. A most unsavoury business, Cribb. Something about indecent photographs she once posed for under a misapprehension that they were commissioned by Lord Leighton. As an aid to his painting, I must make quite clear. If you ask me – and most of London, come to that – there must have been a damned sight more to the blackmail than that, but no matter. Let's not blame the woman for salvaging what she could of her reputation. It is when we come to her account of the murder that the problem arises. You will recall that this obnoxious fellow Perceval was poisoned with cyanide. There was a bottle of the stuff in the poison cabinet of the photographic studio where he worked. It was quite clear that he drank the poison in a glass of madeira. The Home Office analyst found traces in the wine glass and a significant amount in the decanter he had poured it from. Cyanide, Cribb, has the reputation of causing instantaneous death. Where would melodrama villains be without it?' An authoritative note now sounded in the chief inspector's voice. 'The truth of the matter is different. It can take anything from ten to twenty minutes for the victim to die. Instead of dropping dead at once, as his murderer intended, Perceval caused such a rumpus that the servants found him.'

'I remember,' said Cribb. 'Miriam Cromer arrived too late to make it look like suicide.'

'That is what she claims in her confession. Have you studied the confession closely?'

'I wouldn't say "studied", sir. I saw it in the *Daily News*.'

'She states that when Perceval went to lunch she unlocked the poison cabinet, took out the bottle of cyanide and poured a third of the contents into the decanter of madeira. Then she replaced the bottle in the cabinet, locked it again, and went out.'

There was a pause.

'I don't see where the problem is, sir.'

'Presently you will. Consider what happened when Miriam Cromer returned to the house. The dying man had been discovered, the alarm raised and the doctor was already there. He recognised the symptoms of cyanide poisoning' – gratuitously, Jowett said – 'the smell of bitter almonds and the bluish colouring of the skin – and asked Mrs Cromer where the bottle was kept. She states in her confession that she unlocked the cabinet and showed it to him. Now, Sergeant.' Jowett leaned back in the chair with his arms folded. 'I have always had you down as a practical thinker. If Miriam Cromer is to be believed, what would you infer that she needed to possess to carry out her actions?'

Cribb gave a shrug. To be labelled a practical thinker was a back-handed compliment. 'A key?'

'The logical assumption,' Jowett confirmed. 'To put you properly in the picture I should explain that the poison cabinet was nothing like the simple wooden box you and I have in our bathrooms – '

'There's no bathroom here,' Cribb pointed out.

'That has no bearing on it, Sergeant. I was saying that this was a cabinet of German manufacture, built of steel, with a lock no ill-intentioned individual could force. Cromer was admirably responsible about the storage of his chemicals. He was well aware how dangerous cyanide can be and he was determined there should be no accidents. He insisted that all poisonous substances were locked in the cabinet whenever they were not in use. There were two keys. One he kept for himself and wore on his watch-chain with the idea that he would never leave it lying about. It was small and silver in colour and looked quite as handsome on an albert as a lucky sixpence. The other key was given to Perceval. He had it on a key-ring with his personal keys, which he kept in his pocket. They were among the list of articles found on the body. Do you see the significance? If Miriam Cromer is to be believed, on the day she murdered Perceval she was in possession of one of those two keys.'

'Her husband's?' suggested Cribb. 'He was in

40

Brighton, so he wouldn't have wanted it.'

'A reasonable inference,' Jowett said with a tolerant nod. 'She could have slipped it off the watch-chain at some time when Cromer was not wearing his waistcoat, perhaps early in the morning, before he was up. Perfectly possible. Now examine this.' With the air of a conjurer one trick ahead of his audience, Jowett took a piece of paper from an inside pocket and handed it to Cribb.

It was a photo-engraving cut from a magazine. Two men in bowler hats were shown standing at the entrance of what looked like a hotel. The caption read: '*The Annual Conference of the Portrait Photographers' League, at Brighton, on 12th March. The Hon. P. R. Deacon-Pratt, President and Mr H. Cromer, Vice-Chairman.*' The date and Cromer's name were ringed in red ink. More significantly, an arrow had been drawn pointing to the waistcoat of the figure on the right. A key, small, but clearly visible, was shown attached to the watch-chain looped across the front.

'It was cut from the *Photographic Journal* of 24th March,' said Jowett. 'The Home Secretary received it on Monday. It came in an envelope with a West Central postmark. There was no letter of explanation.'

'An explanation isn't necessary,' said Cribb. 'Someone studied Miriam Cromer's confession and remembered this. There's no doubt, I take it, that this *is* one of the keys to the poison cabinet?'

'No doubt whatsoever. The Home Office have

studied it minutely. I saw it myself under magnification and compared it with the key found in Perceval's pocket. The Germans are clever locksmiths, Cribb. That key and its twin were individually cut for the lock on that cabinet. The pattern is intricate, make no mistake. Triple layers of metal, divergent faces – jargon to me, but it means we can eliminate the possibility of a copy having been made.'

'Well, as Cromer was wearing one key on his waistcoat in Brighton, his wife must have opened the cabinet with the other. Is it possible Perceval mislaid it?'

Jowett shook his head. 'I just mentioned, didn't I, that it was on a ring with his other keys. If Perceval had mislaid them, he could not have let himself into the studio that morning. I am assured he did.'

Cribb's mind sifted through possibilities. 'If he removed his jacket while he was working with chemicals –'

'He kept the key-ring in his trouser pocket. It was found there on the body. And we can discount the possibility that she simply asked to borrow his key to the cabinet. That would have alerted him to her intention. She had no conceivable reason for opening the cabinet except to obtain poison. Perceval was no fool, Cribb. He was well aware of the risk he ran in blackmailing her. He was too astute by far to present her with the means of destroying him. Let's not forget, either, that Miriam Cromer claimed to have taken the poison from the cabinet at lunch time, when Perceval was out.

When she saw him next, he was a dead man. If she used Perceval's key to obtain the poison, how did she return it to the pocket of his trousers after he was dead?'

Cribb thought for a moment. 'Just a minute, sir. You said just now that when the doctor asked about poison, Miriam Cromer unlocked the cabinet and showed him the bottle of cyanide. She *must* have had a key in her possession.'

Jowett knocked ash into Cribb's coal-bucket. 'Obviously you are coming to grips with the problem, Sergeant, but the answer isn't there, I'm afraid. You see, I am at a slight advantage here. I have read Dr Eagle's deposition. He states categorically that when he inquired about the cyanide, Mrs Cromer told him the bottle was kept locked in the poison cabinet. He asked to see it and she said she would need Perceval's key to open it. The doctor himself removed the keys from the dead man's trouser pocket. Afterwards he replaced them. The whole thing defies rational explanation.'

'Has anyone asked Miriam Cromer about it?'

'No.'

'Why not? She pleaded guilty. She of all people knows what happened.'

'No, it wouldn't do.'

Cribb rubbed his chin, surprised that a straightforward suggestion should be rejected out of hand.

'She could tell us, yes,' Jowett admitted. 'I cannot fault your logic, Sergeant, but it would be most inappropriate to question Mrs Cromer at this time. Consider her situation. She is condemned to hang twelve days from now. The only thing that can save her is a reprieve. Doubtless she wrote her confession in the hope that it would entitle her to a measure of sympathy. The circumstances of the blackmail were distressing to read, were they not? Here was a decent woman driven to murder through one rather absurd lapse exploited by a vicious blackmailer. On the face of it, there are grounds for mercy. I say on the face of it because her own account is the only one we have. It was accepted by the court because she pleaded guilty and it fitted the available facts. The court had to decide the question of her guilt and she saved them the trouble. Why? In order to give her own account of what happened in the most favourable version possible – else why did she forfeit the right to be defended by an able counsel?'

'It was a gamble, you mean?'

'A gamble for her life, Cribb. At this moment Miriam Cromer is sitting in the condemned cell waiting to see if she has won. Now do you understand why it is out of the question to tackle her about this business of the key? If you or I visited her in Newgate and told her fresh information had come to light, imagine the effect. She would at once conclude that her confession was in doubt – that confession on which she has pinned her hope of a reprieve. It would have a most unsettling effect. The prison staff have difficulty enough calming the minds of the condemned. No, it can't be contemplated, not merely to clarify a detail. The Home Secretary would refuse to sanction it.'

'He wants an explanation just the same.'

'He most certainly does.' A clear note of fear sounded in the Chief Inspector's voice. 'When he understood the significance of this photograph, he called in the Commissioner.'

Cribb's stomach gave a lurch. The Commissioner of the Metropolitan Police was Sir Charles Warren. That impetuous old warhorse had earned his knighthood the year before by putting down a demonstration of the unemployed with a force of four thousand police and six hundred guardsmen. But Bloody Sunday was nothing to his battles since in the offices of Whitehall. He had repeatedly skirmished with the Home Secretary and the Receiver. His own Assistant Commissioner, James Monro, was in open revolt against him. It was common knowledge that each was trying to secure the other's resignation.

Monro was head of the Criminal Investigation Department.

'The Commissioner?'

'Yes, Cribb. I understand why you have gone pale.'

'Isn't this a C.I.D. matter?'

Jowett gave the sigh of a man who had been through this only an hour before. 'I confess that there is a certain difficulty over that. The investigation at Kew was handled by Inspector Waterlow, who is not a member of the C.I.D. The case was so straightforward, with Miriam Cromer the obvious suspect, that our services were not requested.'

'Until this problem cropped up.'

'Yes. The Home Secretary has ordered a new investigation into the circumstances of Perceval's death. He wants it carried out by competent detectives, but in the strictest confidence.'

'That's why you came out to Bermondsey?' said Cribb. 'Why aren't we having this conversation in Mr Monro's office?'

'I had better not answer that question,' Jowett primly said. 'Suffice to say that Sir Charles has assigned me to the case. I shall require your assistance.'

It could not be worse. Monro, the head of C.I.D., had not been informed.

'The situation is delicate, I admit,' Jowett blandly went on. 'As you imply, the Assistant Commissioner is not to be informed at this stage. Knowing how sensitive things are, I made my position clear to Sir Charles. Working as closely as I do to Mr Monro, I could not conceivably carry out a thoroughgoing investigation myself without evincing his interest. As a consequence it was agreed to delegate the day-to-day inquiries to a less conspicuous member of the C.I.D. I nominated you.'

Less conspicuous – Cribb felt entitled to better than that. He did not thank Jowett. 'And where do I stand if Mr Monro gets to hear of this?'

Jowett gave a thin smile. 'Out of earshot, I suggest. To be serious, Sergeant,' he added hastily, 'now that your name has been mentioned to Sir Charles, it would not be in your interest to shrink from the task. By all means request an interview with him if you feel your position is untenable, but I warn you that he may not see it in the same light as yourself. If you were to mention Mr Monro's name in his office, I would not answer for the consequence.'

Through Cribb's burning anger he recognised the truth of this. Jowett's judgment was un-erring when it came to the politics of Scotland Yard. The trap had been sprung and there was no escape. He could accept or resign. Mr Monro would not thank a humble sergeant for making a martyr of himself in the C.I.D. cause. Nor would Millie. From this moment, Cribb's career was vested in Sir Charles Warren, the man the *Pall Mall Gazette* described as *'this hopeless and conspicuous failure.'*

'How do you want me to proceed?'

Jowett's smile reappeared. 'That's the ticket! Well, Sergeant, what it comes down to is whether the confession Miriam Cromer made is reliable. If it isn't, why the devil did she perjure herself to secure a sentence of death? We have eleven days to find an answer. After that the question will be academic, but the Home Secretary will still require a full report. You can leave that to me. The, er, spadework is your responsibility. Be assured that when you need advice it will not be wanting. However, in the circumstances it would not be wise to contact me at Scotland Yard. Better if I get in touch with you in, say, a week from now.' He looked unadmiringly round Cribb's front room. 'This will have to suffice for a rendezvous.'

James Berry was the first to admit that when it came to letter-writing he was no St Paul. It was not the spelling. He had taken a prize once for spelling, in Heckmondwike Dame School. His copperplate was good, too. In the fifties they had taught you well, soon reddened your knuckles when you blotted out a loop. The finest teacher in any school was fear. What Berry had never learnt, because it was not part of the curriculum, was how to find fancy phrases. He liked to come straight out with things.

The letter he had been labouring over for the greater part of three days was now about as elegant as anything he had ever put together. He had started it good and early on purpose, knowing that it would not come quickly. The problem was striking the balance. He needed to make it clear that this was business. He wanted no favours, nor was he giving any. But neither did he wish to seem disrespectful. It was necessary to show he knew he was dealing with a gentleman.

This was how it read:

> *1, Bilton Place,*
> *Bradford*
> *Yorkshire*
> *14th June, 1888*

J. Tussaud, Esq., Proprietor,
Madame Tussaud's Exhibition of Waxworks,
Marylebone Road,
London NW.

Dear Sir,

I have not had the privilege of meeting you, but I understand that the former incumbent of the office I presently hold, namely the late Wm. Marwood, Esq., visited you on a number of occasions and transacted business with you which was a cause of satisfaction on both sides. I am informed that his likeness in wax occupies a place of honour in your exhibition and is an object of interest to the public.

My reason for addressing this communication to your esteemed self is that I have been asked to come to London on or about the 21st inst. in connection with the due enactment of the Law in regard to a case which has received considerable attention in the popular press in recent weeks. I understand that you are accustomed to gratify the public interest in such things by exhibiting the likenesses of certain criminals of note in your Chamber of Horrors. It would seem likely that after the Law has taken its course in the above-mentioned case, you will exhibit a model in wax of the perpetrator of the crime.

I venture to suggest that you must be aware through your dealings with the late Mr Marwood that it has long been a perquisite of the office of executioner to take possession of the clothing last worn by those on whom he has performed his invidious duty. I believe that certain of the models in your exhibition are dressed in the actual clothes of the personages they represent, and that this in no small measure increases the public's curiosity in them. I should

be prepared to discuss the purchase by
Tussaud's of the clothes of the person convicted
in this case should you be interested.

I shall travel to London on Wednesday, 20th
inst., and I could, if you desire, attend your
office the following morning to discuss the
matter. Should you care to meet me, your con-
firmation by letter will oblige.

Your humble servant,
James Berry

He was in two minds about 'Your humble
servant'. He was not looking for charity. He was
in a position to state terms. He had waited long
enough for a chance like this. Not one of his
clients had been a candidate for Tussaud's until
now. Not one in four years. Bill Marwood had
been luckier – Charlie Peace, Kate Webster, Dr
Lamson. No wonder they had made a waxwork
of Marwood himself, when he had turned off
notables like that.

There was no need to reach a decision yet
about how to end the letter. It would have to
wait until he heard something definite from the
Sheriff of London. Then he would copy it out
in his best hand and decide whether he wanted
to remain a humble servant.

What mattered more was the price. He was
thinking he might ask twenty for the clothes,
which was twice what the Sheriff would pay for
the hanging. Twenty was not exorbitant when
you reckoned the numbers who would pay to
look at the figure.

Twenty would cover the cost of what he had in mind to do in London and leave some to spare.

The prisoner Cromer was a deep one, her wardresses had decided. They had confidently expected trouble from her when the truth of her situation had sunk in. The way it took prisoners was variable; all you could count on was that there would be incidents in the first forty-eight hours, anything from fainting-fits to assaults on the staff. The doctor generally gave them something. If they were bad enough they were put in the infirmary for a spell. Once the first crisis was over, they would weep for a day or two and then begin to come to terms with their sentence. Provided visitors did not excite them, they were manageable after that. Passive almost to the finish. A few actually went to that without a murmur.

Cromer had given no indication of mental turmoil. She appeared to be in command of herself. It was as if Newgate had not touched her yet. In prison uniform, the coarse blue jacket and limp linsey skirt, the plain white mob cap with close-fitting frills, she should have looked like any other felon. She did not. She was different.

The clothes fitted well enough. She wore the cap exactly as prescribed, with the ends tied in a bow under her chin. If a strand of gold hair slipped loose she was swiftly ordered to tuck it out of sight. Her sleeves were neatly rolled in regulation fashion. Really there was small scope for self-expression in the uniform, and any signs of it were soon corrected.

Her strangeness was of a more elusive kind, not definable as a breach of prison regulations, but flagrant in a way that offended the wardresses because they were not able to exercise control over it. She accepted the restrictions, the indignities, the scrubbing-brush and the latrine-bucket, without a syllable of protest. She was scrupulously subordinate in her dealings with the staff. Yet she remained remote. The privations should have made her increasingly dependent on her gaolers; it was a process so predictable that they took it as a right. Deprived of it, they could not understand how this prisoner could be simultaneously submissive and indifferent. Certainly there were indications of strain in her features, but she persisted in her aloofness. Her eyes showed no more interest in her attendants than the furniture or the walls.

The governor had noticed it. On Monday, Cromer's fourth day in Newgate, he had asked for her to be brought to his rooms as was his custom with newly admitted prisoners. Hawkins and Bell had taken her. It meant walking to the other end of the prison through low stone passages, relics of the eighteenth century, never progressing far before an iron-bolted door had to be unlocked and slammed with a resounding crash after they were through.

There was a door beyond which you found yourself stepping on carpet instead of stone. Far from producing an impression of comfort, it was so alien to the rest of Newgate that it disturbed even the wardresses. Bell's knees turned to jelly every time.

In the carpeted passage they stopped at a panelled oak door with brass fittings polished to military standard. It was Hawkins who knocked.

'Enter.'

The governor's room was vast. Vast, that is, compared with cells thirteen feet by seven and corridors so narrow that in places two people could not pass without one stepping aside. The sense of space was unnerving.

It was panelled in dark wood and furnished with high-backed leather chairs. There were bookshelves to the ceiling, pictures of hunting scenes, stuffed animals' heads and green velvet curtains. It was warm, so there was no fire burning. The governor was facing a tapestry firescreen.

'If you please, sir, the prisoner Cromer,' the less nervous wardress announced from the doorway.

'Yes.' He turned, a grey-haired man with a waxed moustache and blue, watery eyes. 'Step forward, Cromer.' His voice was strange to the ear, modulated by carpets and furnishings.

The prisoner took two steps towards him.

'Over here, if you please. I may be fearsome, but I am not dangerous, I assure you.'

The wardresses watched her approach to within a yard of him, her face raised to meet his. She was not fearful. Not in the least.

'I make a point of seeing each prisoner who enters Newgate,' he told her in a voice just audible across the room, 'and I always begin by making it clear that this institution and others like it exist only to meet the requirements of the law. For that reason I shall say nothing about the events that brought you here. They were the subject of your trial and I imagine you would not care to be reminded of them. My responsibility is to see that the sentence of the law is carried out – to a point, that is. The ultimate responsibility rests with the Sheriff of the City of London. If your sentence is confirmed by Her Majesty I shall be required to deliver you to the Sheriff for the implementation of that sentence. A formality that you need not concern yourself with, unless it comforts you to know that we in Newgate are responsible only for your custody, not, do you understand . . . ?'

'I understand.'

Bell caught her breath. The prisoner had failed to address him properly.

The governor fingered the knot of his necktie. 'You will wish to know how long you may expect to spend in Newgate. The period prescribed by the Home Office is a little over two weeks. Three Sundays must elapse since the day on which sentence was passed. Assuming there is no intervention' – he crossed the room to his desk – 'I must deliver you to the Sheriff shortly before eight in the morning on, er . . .' He picked up a piece of paper and studied it.

'Monday, 25th June,' said the prisoner.

There was a sepulchral silence in the room. The governor put down the paper and stood looking at her. From his expression, he was more surprised than annoyed by the interruption. He returned to the fireplace. 'Doubtless you are resting your hopes on a reprieve.' His eyes turned to a small plaster bust that stood on the mantelpiece. 'The Sovereign has been known on occasions to exercise clemency on the recommendation of the Secretary of State for the Home Office. My advice to you, for what it is worth, is to put all such thoughts out of your mind. I have had the unhappy duty of meeting a considerable number of people in circumstances identical to yours at this moment. I have observed that those who endure the experience best are the ones who reconcile themselves to meeting their Maker. The prison chaplain, Father Hughes, is already known to you. I urge you to be guided by his spiritual advice. You are a member of the Church, I trust?'

She nodded.

'Good. Then I hope you will unburden your soul to him.'

She said nothing. She had said nothing, either, to the chaplain each time he had visited her in the cell. The tracts he had given her were unopened. The wardresses knew and no doubt the governor knew as well, but he did not press the matter.

'You may also receive visits from your next of kin. That would include your husband, father, mother – '

'My parents are dead.'

'Cromer, it is customary to address me as "sir". I am sorry about your parents. However, it must be a consolation that they were spared the distress of this time. If you have brothers or sisters – '

'Sir,' she said in a steady voice, 'I have no desire to see them in this place. My husband, yes. I believe I am also entitled to visits from my solicitor.'

The governor distractedly groomed his moustache. 'Indeed, I was coming to that, but I caution you again that it is most unwise to base any hope on a judicial release from your sentence. Is there any other matter you wish to raise with me?'

'Not for the present, sir.'

'There will be opportunities, anyway, of speaking to me again.'

With that, the governor had gestured to them to lead her away. Before they had closed the door he had gone to a cupboard and taken out a whisky glass.

FRIDAY, 15th JUNE

Cribb had slept badly. His brain had floundered for hours in the shallows of oblivion, producing aberrations that jerked him awake. Once he was being ushered in by Jowett to Sir Charles Warren, but instead of the Commissioner at his desk, there was a camera facing them and the little figure that emerged from under the black cloth was female and grey-haired and wearing a crown. He had sat up in bed with such a start that it had disturbed Millie. He had not told her his dream. Instead he had gone to make tea and when he returned with the cup he had distracted her by suggesting they plan a visit to the theatre. He had known she would rise to that. *The Mascotte* at the Haymarket with Miss Lottie Piper. Millie was so quick with the suggestion that they both laughed. Later, in the darkness, Cribb was troubled. She had not asked him the reason for Jowett's visit. He had always been frank with Millie. It was as if he was buying her silence for the price of two theatre tickets.

He knew if she heard about this she would jump to the wrong conclusion. She would think the Commissioner had singled him out because he was the best detective in the force. Millie had never doubted it, always believed they were on the point of promoting him. It was no use telling her Warren had gone to Jowett because he was the Judas of Monro's team and Jowett in a blue fit had blurted the first name that sprang to his lips.

Cribb was a realist. After seventeen years on a sergeant's rank, it would take fireworks on the Crystal Palace scale to get him lifted.

He had decided to start with Inspector Waterlow. When he looked up the address of the police station at Kew he found an asterisk against the entry. The footnote below stated *Not continuously manned.* A memory of Waterlow as a constable excusing himself from the beat flitted into Cribb's mind. He drew a long breath, picked up the valise containing the papers on the Cromer case and walked out of Scotland Yard with a maltreated look in his eye.

He took a train from Waterloo on the London and South Western.

He was the only passenger to alight at Kew Gardens. The platform was deserted. Nobody collected his ticket. It was a good thing he needed no help with directions. The address was Station Approach.

Before leaving the booking hall his eye caught a name among the posters advertising local businesses.

HOWARD CROMER
PHOTOGRAPHIC ARTIST
PARK LODGE, KEW GREEN

The highest class of photographs reproduced under ordinary conditions of light. Sittings by appointment. Portraits, cabinet and carte-de-visite, family groups and wedding parties a speciality.

58

In pencil, somebody had added *Funerals Arranged.*

Station Approach was broad and shaded by trees. The police station was located above a chemist's. Access was up an iron staircase at the side. Cribb opened a door badly in need of paint.

'Good day, sir,' said a tall, callow constable holding a large ginger cat in his arms. 'Not a bad day at all. Capital for Ascot. What can we do for you?'

'You can tell Inspector Waterlow, if he is in, that Sergeant Cribb of Statistics would like a word with him.'

The cat was dropped like a stone.

'Statistics. Yes, Sergeant. Very good. I'll tell him this minute.' He opened a door behind the desk just enough to put his head and shoulder round. A murmured, agitated exchange took place. He closed the door and turned back to Cribb. 'The Inspector won't be a moment, Sergeant.' He busied himself with some pieces of paper.

'This your animal?' Cribb inquired. The cat was leaning on his shins.

'Just a stray, Sergeant,' the constable answered unconvincingly. 'We get a lot of them, being next to the butcher's. When you came in, I was ascertaining whether it had a collar, for identification.'

'I hope you've got it in the occurrence book,' said Cribb tartly.

A bald head and shoulders appeared round the door, hands fastening the top buttons of an

59

inspector's tunic. 'Cribb, it really is you,' said Inspector Waterlow. 'What are you waiting there for? Come inside, man.'

The cat was inside first. It hopped on to the window sill and settled proprietorially in the sun. Inspector Waterlow made no attempt to remove it.

Slimly built, with ferocious eyebrows to compensate for baldness, he had altered little in the ten years since Cribb had seen him. The set of his head on an overlong, narrow neck still unaccountably irked.

'Stoke Newington, wasn't it?' he said unnecessarily. 'By George, a lot of water has gone under the bridge since those days. Busy times. Sit down, won't you? Have a spell in the armchair. I don't suppose you get much time for that. Where are you now?'

The chair was warm from a recent sitter. 'The Yard. Statistics Branch, sir.' Some evasion was necessary with Waterlow.

'Out of the action, then? My word, you've earned a turn behind a desk if anyone has. Do you mean to say they haven't made you up to inspector yet?'

'I had two commendations a couple of years back. That's all.'

'Good man,' said Inspector Waterlow, more to the cat than Cribb. He was stroking its head with his forefinger. 'Confidentially, promotion in the force is a lottery, old boy. I'm the first to admit I was no great shakes as a copper. Got my name mentioned in the right quarters just the same – hang it, there had to be *some* compensation for all the paper-work I did. Soon after you left, I got my stripes. But I didn't see myself as a sergeant, so I er' – he removed his forefinger from the cat and tapped the side of his head – 'submitted a practical suggestion to the Commissioner: to give up issuing truncheon-cases and have a truncheon-pocket sewn into the uniform instead. As you know, it was acted upon two years ago, and I was made up to inspector.'

'Doesn't sound like a lottery to me.'

'You're right. I owe it to my inventive mind,' said Waterlow smugly.

'Where did you go as inspector?'

Waterlow grinned sheepishly. 'I did a rather calamitous tour of duty at Bow Street. After that they sent me to Kew. I must say, I find it more agreeable than central London.'

Cribb murmured agreement from the armchair and pondered the vagaries of fate.

'What brings you here?' Waterlow casually inquired. 'No problem over my statistics, I hope? There isn't a great amount of crime here, you will appreciate. A few incidents in the Royal Botanic Gardens – pilfering orchids, and so forth. We had an indecent exposure in the Water Lily House last month, but I can't in all conscience say we make many arrests. The most exciting thing in years was the poisoning in Kew Green last spring. No doubt you heard. I sorted it out myself. The wife did it, of course. She confessed before the trial. Facing facts, you see. By then I had a cast-iron case against her.'

'Nice work, sir.' Cribb beamed at Waterlow.

This was the opening he needed. 'As it happens, the Kew Green poisoning is what brings me out here. Someone in the Yard has the notion that we could detect crime more efficiently if we kept a fuller record of felonies committed in the past. As you know, the present practice is to list the number of felonies committed under different headings – housebreaking, robbery with violence, arson and so on. That's a help, but it doesn't tell us what *time* most burglaries are committed, or what class of person raises fires.'

'Is that important?'

'It could be useful, sir. We don't know if it's feasible yet. Between ourselves, it's going to mean the devil of a lot of work in Statistics Branch. Be that as it may, I've been asked to see if I can get the salient facts about a crime and reduce them to a row of columns. If we can get our columns right, we can do anything in Statistics. I'm starting with murder. From all I've heard, your Kew Green case was a copybook investigation.'

Waterlow went pink. 'Oh, I wouldn't go so far as that. It's decent of you to say so, of course.'

'A classic of its kind,' eulogised Cribb. 'Ideal for my purpose. You won't find it tedious telling me how you nabbed Mrs Miriam Cromer?'

Benignly, Waterlow answered, 'I am gratified to know that my little investigation is of any consequence.'

'The cornerstone, so far as I am concerned,' said Cribb, seeing there was no limit to the flattery Waterlow could absorb. 'Will it trouble you, sir, if I take notes?'

'Not in the least. Where would you like to begin?'

'At the point when the police were called to the house. I understand you personally were the first member of the force on the scene.'

'Yes, I had a hand in this from the outset,' Waterlow confirmed, and his voice took on the compelling tone of the anecdotist with a good tale to tell. 'It was a Monday afternoon in March, towards five o'clock, a fine day, as I remember, still light. I was clipping my front hedge. I have my own house in Maze Road, if you follow, and I generally take Monday afternoon to catch up on my gardening. The station is not continuously manned, thank Heaven. There I was, then, tidying up the privet, when a girl in servant's dress came running up the road and told me I was wanted urgently at Park Lodge. Fortunately Dr Eagle knows my habits and sent the girl direct to my house with the news that the man Perceval was dead. It's a matter of two or three minutes from Maze Road to Kew Green, so I was there directly. When I arrived, Eagle was attending to Mrs Cromer in her room. It seems she had passed out from the shock. I went straight to the processing room where the body was. All in all, Cribb, my career has not brought me face to face with death too often, but I saw at once that Perceval had not gone peacefully. The poor fellow had kicked off a shoe and torn his clothes in his agony, besides rucking up the carpet and knocking over a chair. I found a wine glass lying on its side on the floor, so the possibility of poison suggested itself to me even before Dr Eagle came in and gave his diagnosis. He's an old stager, you know, sharp as a winkle-pin. "Hold on to that glass," he said. "I'll stake my reputation there's cyanide in it." He took me to the poison cabinet and showed me the bottle of the stuff, more than half empty.'

'Was the cabinet unlocked?'

'No. We had to take the keys out of the dead man's pocket to get the damned thing open. But old Eagle told me he had already had the cabinet open once. As soon as he had sniffed the cyanide, the old boy had asked Miriam Cromer where it was kept. She had shown him. He had to take the keys out of Perceval's trouser pocket for her to unlock the cabinet. You know, that struck me as peculiar at the time, that a man committing suicide would put the poison bottle back in the cabinet and lock it again. Anyway, after Dr Eagle had checked the contents of the cabinet he locked it and put the keys back in the pocket, to leave the scene of the crime exactly as he found it. For my benefit, you see.'

'And you presumed it was a case of suicide?'

'Just as you would have done, Sergeant,' said Waterlow, piqued. 'Perceval had been alone in the studio all afternoon. But make a note of this for your columns. I took possession of the wine glass and the poison for analysis, and – most importantly, as it turned out – the three decanters. They weren't in an obvious position, you know. I found them locked in a small sideboard – chiffonier, I remember they called it in court. Two days later I heard from the analyst

that the madeira was laced with cyanide. It quite
transformed the course of my inquiry. Up to
then I had taken it that Perceval had done away
with himself. I was busy collecting evidence
about his financial affairs. He was in deep with
the bookies at the time of his death. Seventy
pounds, give or take a few. That's half a year's
wages for a fellow in his job.'

'Mine, too.'

Waterlow was too deep in his narrative to
take note of Cribb's admission. 'Plenty have
committed suicide for less. I think it would have
satisfied a coroner's jury. But once I heard there
was poison in the decanter, I had to ask myself
what could account for that. Am I going too
fast?'

'I'm keeping up,' said Cribb. 'You realised
someone else was responsible for the poisoning.'

'Exactly. If Perceval had poisoned himself, he
wouldn't have put cyanide in the decanter. He
would have put it straight into the wine glass.
There was no question of it, Cribb – I had a
case of murder on my hands. That's a devil of
a thing to discover when you're the man in
charge of a station, with other responsibilities
and precious little assistance. Possibly I should
have asked the C.I.D. for help, but, dash it, I
didn't want the Yard taking over my office. And
candidly I considered I was capable of handling
the case myself. As I saw it, the murderer had to
be a member of the household at Park Lodge.
Already I had checked that there were no visitors on the day of the murder. Mr Howard
Cromer was in Brighton. Unless he had tam-

pered with the decanter before he left, only his wife or the servants could have done it. I made an appointment to visit Park Lodge, asking that every member of the household should be available to answer questions.' Waterlow gave a sigh. 'In retrospect, I can see that I should not have let them know that I was coming.'

'Was someone not available?'

'No, they were all present, but so was Allingham, the family solicitor. I would have got a lot more done without him. He knows his job, does young Allingham. I had met him already on the day of the murder. He was present when I interviewed Miriam Cromer the first time. I believe Dr Eagle had sent for him, the wily old cove. Well, on this occasion Allingham raised so many objections to my questions that he came close to obstructing me in the course of my duty. You may find this difficult to believe, but it took over an hour to establish who had filled the blasted decanter, and at what time.'

'Miriam Cromer?'

Waterlow nodded. 'By sheer persistence I managed to extract the information. She admitted it was a regular task of hers – responsibility, she called it – filling the decanters after the wine arrived on Monday mornings. By Friday they were empty, so there was a standing order with the wine merchant. On the day of the murder the wine arrived at noon and she went with it to the studio as usual.'

'Was Perceval working there?'

'So she told me. In the next room, the processing room, where the poison cabinet was situated. It was obvious that she couldn't have obtained the cyanide while he was working there – if she was telling the truth. As Perceval was dead, I could not confirm the statement. Clever. The solicitor made damned sure she didn't say any more. Anything else would have to be discovered by patient detective work.'

'Did you question the others, sir?'

'Yes. I told you Cromer spent the day in Brighton at a conference. The three servants, all females, didn't venture upstairs until they felt they couldn't ignore the racket Perceval was making in his convulsions. Cromer doesn't like his clients to see the domestics, so they were supposed to keep below stairs. By the time they got to him, the poor beggar was paralysed and bereft of speech. That's about all I got from the servants, except the alibis they provided for each other. Oh, they did confirm that there wasn't a visitor to the house all day, apart from tradesmen. There was only one conclusion I could draw, and that was that Miriam Cromer was a murderess.' Waterlow paused for dramatic effect. 'You can imagine my predicament, Cribb. Here was a respectable married woman of the genteel class, or not far short of it. Their neighbours are people like the Duchess of Cambridge. A Major-General lives next door and the Director-General of Kew Gardens is close by. You can't ask people of that class whether they have noticed anything irregular.'

'You must have gone back to the servants.'

'Yes, I'm coming to that,' Waterlow peevishly said. 'I did, and I don't mind telling you that I managed it without creating the least suspicion in the family. Two of the servants lived in, but a third, a housemaid of thirteen named Margaret Booth, resided in Brentford. "Resided" isn't quite the word now that I recall the squalor of the street, but that's of no importance. Margaret had been warned by Allingham in peril of her job not to make a statement of any kind to the police.' He gave a belly-laugh. 'Young Margaret wasn't prepared for me to be seated in her own parlour beside her father when she came home. The old man describes himself as a docker. If you ask me, the only dock he regularly sees is the one at Brentford Police Court. He is habitually drunk. I was lucky to find him vertical, more or less, when I picked him up at the pub on the corner. By the time his daughter Margaret came home, I made sure Albert Booth was a sober and frightened man, and so was his wife. They were convinced I would get him sent down for three months' hard if I didn't get co-operation. Margaret's resistance didn't last long. She gave me what I wanted: a tolerable account of Miriam Cromer and her dealings with Josiah Perceval.'

'She knew about the blackmail, did she?'

'Lord, no, nothing so helpful as that. She told me that it was no secret below stairs that Mrs Cromer had a strong dislike for Perceval. Nobody knew why exactly, just that it had got worse in recent weeks. There were sometimes arguments upstairs when Mr Cromer was out, and Perceval seemed to get the better of them, which surprised the servants. They had thought

of their mistress as iron-willed, more than a
match for the likes of Perceval. What was said
was not audible in the servants' quarters, but
they could tell when voices were raised, and they
also knew by the state of Mrs Cromer's eyes
when she had been reduced to tears. That was
as much as I got from Margaret Booth about
what went on upstairs, but' – Waterlow beamed
in self-congratulation – 'I persuaded her to talk
about the other servants.'

Cribb tried to appear impressed. Waterlow in
the old days had put in less time on the beat
than anyone at Stoke Newington. The titbits
of gossip any bright young constable picked up
automatically from making conversation at door-
ways were outside his experience. He had never
been invited in for a slice of rabbit pie in his
life. So it was a triumph to have coaxed a few
confidences from Margaret Booth. Cribb listened and made an occasional note. He could
raise no interest in how the housekeeper em-
bezzled the accounts and what the parlourmaid
got up to with the grocer's boy. He wanted to
know about Miriam Cromer.

What was she like, this woman who would
hang unless he found a flaw in her confession?
In any regular investigation he would have
started by interviewing her, forming an impression of her character. There was more to detective work than clues and statements. It involved
people, their ambitions and fears, innocence and
guilt. You needed solid evidence to determine
the truth, but you could divine a lot by meeting
them face to face. Whatever had happened that

afternoon in Park Lodge, the question for Cribb was whether Miriam Cromer had done what she claimed. She was the focus of his investigation, but because authority deemed it inappropriate he was prevented from meeting her. He was obliged to glean what he could at second hand, from people whose recollection would be coloured by their own conceits and prejudices. Waterlow was the first.

'When I visited the house that evening to put my information to practical use,' the self-advertisement ran on, 'I used the tradesmen's entrance, naturally. Nobody upstairs knew I was making a second visit to Park Lodge. I relied on what I knew to keep the servants' tongues from wagging.'

'What did the housekeeper tell you?' Cribb asked, his patience on the ebb.

Waterlow smacked his lips. 'She was a frightened woman before I was through, I can tell you, Cribb. What did I learn from her? Why, the very thing I needed: the dates when Mrs Cromer had gone into the studio to talk to Perceval and their raised voices had been heard downstairs. She knew exactly when it happened because the meetings took place when the master of the house was out for the day and not expected back till late in the evening. She has to keep a note of his days out to get her catering right. She keeps a calendar in the kitchen on which such things are marked. There were four occasions between October and March when Mrs Cromer and Perceval had a "ruction", as she called it. I noted them carefully in my pocket-book.'

'What form did these ructions take?' asked Cribb.

'There was a difference of opinion about that. Everyone in the servants' quarters agreed that there were raised voices, and the parlourmaid told me Mrs Cromer was reduced to tears, but the housekeeper insisted that they never heard weeping. She said the mistress was red-eyed with anger. I think she was probably right. I don't see Miriam Cromer dabbing her eyes with a lace handkerchief, do you?'

'I haven't met the lady.'

Waterlow accepted this with a nod. 'Well, as I say, I preferred to believe the housekeeper, but the parlourmaid did give me another piece of information that I put to good use. She had twice observed that on days after these scenes her mistress went out for a morning walk. There may seem nothing remarkable to you in that, Sergeant, but it was a departure from normal practice. She was in the habit of taking a daily constitutional in the Botanic Gardens. This is where local knowledge came in useful. The Gardens being part of my patch, I happen to know that they don't open in the morning. One o'clock till sunset are the hours. I asked the parlourmaid if she had observed which direction Mrs Cromer had taken. She told me she had watched from the breakfast room. She was interested, because it was such an uncommon thing. Mrs Cromer had walked up to the main road and turned right, towards Kew Bridge.'

Waterlow grinned again. 'A stroll by the Thames? Feeding the ducks? Not on your life. She was going to Brentford to put jewellery in pawn, and I proved it!'

'How did you get on to that, sir?'

'Smart detective work. I told you just now that Perceval was in trouble with the book-makers at the time of his death. Well, he had been running up debts for a year or more. He made occasional repayments to show good faith. He dealt with Harry Cobb's, the Richmond firm. I went to see them and took a note of those repayments, the dates and sums involved. I compared them with the dates the housekeeper had given me, and, what do you know, they matched! It was obvious what the connection was: Perceval had persuaded Mrs Cromer to help him meet his debts, except that persuasion didn't come in to it. As I discovered from the housekeeper, the lady of the house had precious little ready money of her own. She didn't need it. Women of her class don't spend money. They have accounts, which their husbands settle quarterly. They keep a few shillings in their purse for emergencies, but nothing like the money Perceval was getting – twelve, fifteen pounds. To lay her hands on as much of the ready as that, she would need to go to a bank or a moneylender. I verified that she had no account of her own.' Waterlow waved his hand expansively. 'So she must have raised a loan, and that's where local knowledge came in again. The nearest pawnshop is in Brentford High Street.' He counted on his fingers. 'Four visits.

October, December, January, February. All confirmed by the pawnbroker. Jewellery each time. Good stuff, too, that could have raised more, but she was glad to take the first price he offered. He would have made a splendid prosecution witness, that pawnbroker. He gave me a first-rate description, from her plush hat to her brown buttoned boots.'

'So you concluded Perceval was blackmailing her?'

'Proved it,' said Waterlow. 'I even recovered the pawn-tickets, ready to exhibit in court. The only thing I didn't fathom was what he had on her. I must admit that vulgar pictures never crossed my mind. I mean it doesn't square with High Church and a house on Kew Green. It doesn't square at all.'

'So much the better for a touch of blackmail,' Cribb commented.

Grudgingly, Waterlow agreed. 'But it's not the sort of thing you expect from the daughter of a mayor of Hampstead,' he went on. 'If a well-bred woman has a secret, nine times out of ten it's a lover. You have to have a theory to work on, don't you? The walks she took in the Botanic Gardens interested me. I would have put my money on some sort of assignation among the rhododendrons. As a matter of fact, I had practically convinced myself it was young Allingham, the solicitor. He is more of her own generation than her husband. Did you know that she is sixteen years younger than Cromer? Allingham's connection with the family goes back a few years, I gather. He was in the social set they moved in before the marriage. He is the only one they have kept up with, I suppose because of the professional connection. It still seemed to me – and, I think, the housekeeper, who is a shrewd woman – that Mr Simon Allingham was taking a closer interest in Miriam Cromer than you would expect from the family solicitor. There was nothing you could describe as flagrant, simply looks that passed between them and the way he put his hand on her arm to prevent her answering my questions.' He shrugged. 'I have to admit to a slight misjudgment there. As I say, the real reason for the blackmail took me by surprise.' Having admitted his fallibility, Waterlow absolved himself. 'That's of no importance. I'm sure we would have secured a conviction on the evidence we had. The prosecution didn't need to go into the details of the blackmail. In fact, it could have been detrimental to the case to dwell on the business. All in all, I believe I was entitled to expect a commendation in court for the work I did.'

Cribb was near the limit of his tolerance, but he still had one crucial question to put. 'As a matter of interest, what sort of person is Miriam Cromer?'

Waterlow blinked, jogged out of his train of thought. 'You seem to be taking this job seriously, Cribb. I thought it was statistics you came to ask me about.'

With an effort to be amiable, Cribb said, 'You've got me interested in the case, I can't

74

deny it, sir. Miriam Cromer makes a fascinating study. A woman who will kill is a rare one.'

'Rare — my word, yes.' Inspector Waterlow perched himself on the edge of his desk and took the cat into his lap, stroking it as he talked. 'Exquisitely good-looking. Entirely in command. Questions wouldn't shake her. Look how she stood up in court and faced old Colbeck when he sentenced her to death. I tell you, he was paler than she was. An astonishing woman by any reckoning. To be candid, I have a secret hope that the Home Secretary will commute the sentence to penal servitude for life. Miriam Cromer is altogether too remarkable to consign to the hangman's rope. There's a world of difference between a woman like her and that creature in Richmond a year or two ago who murdered her employer and boiled her body in the copper.'

'Kate Webster? No comparison, sir.'

'You know, I'm still unable to understand what induced Miriam Cromer to confess. The case I put together was overwhelming, I admit, but a decent counsel, Sir Charles Russell, for instance — the family could afford him, for God's sake — might have raised points that would have helped towards a reprieve. As it stands, there's simply her confession. I can't believe the prospect of a long trial unnerved her. Whatever she is, she is no coward.'

'Possibly she reckoned it would save her from the gallows,' Cribb suggested. 'A frank admission of guilt is something in a prisoner's favour.'

'Not in the eyes of the law. The details of the

crime in her own words are very damning. It was not an impulsive crime. She planned it. There's little doubt she would have got away with it if the cyanide had killed the victim instantaneously, as she expected. She could have let herself into the studio when she got back to the house and calmly emptied that decanter and refilled it with fresh madeira. To make quite sure, she could have placed the cyanide bottle beside the corpse. There's no denying it was done in cold blood, Cribb. The judge made that clear when he sentenced her. Having met her, I believe I understand how she planned it and carried it through. If you ask me what sets her apart from other women, it's an absence of pity. She is so damned self-possessed that she can't imagine how other people feel. In all the interviews I had with her, she never expressed a syllable of sympathy for her victim. I'd lay all the money I own that even in the death cell she isn't wasting a thought on Perceval.'

'From all accounts, he isn't worth it,' said Cribb. 'She sounds a lot more interesting than her victim. Like you, sir, I find it difficult to understand why a woman of her character should have confessed. Did she make the confession to you?'

'No, it was done while she was awaiting trial in Newgate. She drew it up with the solicitor, Allingham, and then arrangements were made for her to swear an affidavit before a magistrate. Everyone was taken by surprise. Cheated, you could say. This had every promise of being one of the classic trials of the century.'

Cribb thought, *with Inspector Waterlow of V Division as principal witness for the prosecution.* 'Yes, sir, it must have been a facer after all the work you put in. To see it written down in a confession, all that evidence you spent weeks patiently uncovering. Cruel.' He solemnly shook his head. Then he said more brightly, 'I expect it wasn't wasted. You still had to check that the confession was true.'

'That wasn't difficult,' said Waterlow. 'The evidence confirmed everything she said. You couldn't fault it.'

'I'm sure.' Cribb paused, about to venture into a sensitive area. 'You said just now that the reason for the blackmail took you by surprise.'

'The indecent pictures? That's true.'

'Did you by any chance turn up any of these pictures when you looked through Perceval's possessions, sir?'

Waterlow gave a sly grin. 'Care to see one, then? No, Cribb, I didn't. He sold her the ones he had, and she destroyed them. If you recall, she said in the confession he was offering to buy the plates. £150, wasn't it?'

'So there were no pictures or plates in Perceval's lodgings?'

'I told you, no. It isn't important,' added Waterlow. 'The details of the blackmail are immaterial. The fact that blackmail took place is admitted, and there is plenty of proof. From the moment I walked into the pawnbroker's in Brentford we had Miriam Cromer on toast.'

'No wonder she confessed,' said Cribb, content to resume the adulation now that the point was clear.

'I was sorry when it came to an end,' said Waterlow. 'I don't often get challenges here in Kew, but I'm capable of meeting them. Tell them that at Scotland Yard if you like. While they collect statistics, we in the divisions are out on the streets coping with crime from hour to hour.'

When Cribb got up to go, Inspector Waterlow took his place in the armchair. Justifiably, Cribb reflected when he got outside. The streets of Kew were as deserted as when he had arrived.

'I represent Mrs Miriam Cromer. My name is Allingham.'

The governor put down his pen to look at the solicitor. Twenty-seven, no more, he guessed. Well turned out, in a light grey suit and purple waistcoat with matching cravat. Black boots and gaiter with white buttons. Hat and valise in hand. Straw-coloured hair, parted and brushed close to the head. An intelligent face, blue-eyed, clean-shaven, distinctly hostile in expression.

'Won't you sit down, Mr Allingham? There is nothing untoward, I hope?'

'I have come from visiting Mrs Cromer.'

'You found her well?'

'Considering the circumstances, yes.'

'Our observation is that she is well in control of herself, Mr Allingham. She appears to have an inner strength that belies her somewhat frail physique.'

'Governor, I wish to protest at the visiting facilities. It is quite impossible to conduct a conversation through an iron grille with two prison officers at my client's shoulder.'

If that was the objection, it would soon be remedied. When the Sheriff's warrant arrived, the prisoner would be moved to the condemned wing, where cell visiting was the rule. If Allingham's manner had been a shade more civil, the governor would have mentioned this at once. 'I am sorry you find it inconvenient. It is the usual arrangement. There are regulations we are obliged to conform with, Mr Allingham. I have some two hundred other prisoners in my charge who meet their visitors under similar circumstances. What precisely is the problem?'

Allingham made a sound of impatience. 'This is a woman under sentence of death. She is entitled to consultations with her solicitor. I have documents I wished to discuss with her. I was prevented even from passing them under the grille for her to inspect.'

'Which documents were these?'

'A copy of the petition which is being addressed to the Home Secretary. And yesterday's edition of *The Times*.'

'What bearing, may I inquire, does *The Times* have on the case?'

'There were two letters pertaining to the trial. I wanted my client to read them.'

The governor had seen them. Both were sent in protest at the sentence passed on the prisoner. One was from the Howard Association. The other was from a man named Morgan Browne who wrote to the newspapers every time a woman was sentenced to death.

'Prisoners are not permitted to read newspapers, Mr Allingham.'

'Dammit, she needs to know what is being done on her behalf.'

'I am sure you will have acquainted her with that information. As to the visiting arrangements,' the governor went on, 'you may anticipate some improvement there. When do you next intend to visit?'

'Tomorrow. I come each day.'

'It may well be possible for you to visit the prisoner in a cell. Tomorrow or the next day.'

Allingham nodded, under the impression he had secured a concession. 'And the wardresses?'

'There I cannot help. Home Office regulations state that two officers must attend the prisoner day and night.'

'She tells me that the light in the cell is not put out at night. Sleep is extremely difficult for her.'

The governor nodded. 'She has mentioned that to me. Unfortunately that is another regulation which is quite unalterable. I recommended her to place a dark handkerchief over her eyes when she wishes to sleep. Believe me, Mr Allingham, I have no desire to subject her to undue suffering. It would help considerably if she could be persuaded to speak to the chaplain. She seems most reluctant to confide in him. He is a man of considerable experience in fortifying prisoners under sentence of death, but he tells me he has found her quite intractable. If you or her husband could possibly convey to Mrs Cromer – '

'That would be like telling her we are abandoning hope!' said Allingham in a shocked voice.

'On the contrary. The hope of redemption – '

'Hope of a *reprieve*,' Allingham broke in. 'That is what is keeping her from despair.'

There was a silence of several seconds.

'If I may offer you some advice,' the governor told the young man, 'you are doing your client no service by encouraging such expectations. It only defers the moment when she must come to terms with reality, but it makes that moment infinitely harder to bear. She should be using this time to fortify herself for what she must face nine days from now.'

Allingham went pale. 'She will not die. They would not dare hang her.'

'I have received no indications to the contrary, Mr Allingham.'

The solicitor started up from his chair, came to the desk and gripped it with his hand. He seemed on the point of saying something, then thought better of it and withdrew his hand.

To cover the awkwardness between them, the governor said, 'If I hear anything from the Home Office, you may be sure I shall inform you.'

Allingham, tight-lipped, said, 'You will, sir. I assure you of that.'

In the largest photograph, dominating the wall facing the door, she was standing against a plain backcloth. There was no rustic gate, no chairback for her hand to rest on. The pose was three-quarter length. Austere in a dark dress buttoned to the neck, she stood stiff-backed, hands lightly clasped in front, head tilted a little, eyes focused above the camera. Her left side was in shadow, the features picked out sharply. There was no concession in the photography; the beauty was all her own.

Cribb studied the face minutely. He had quickly taken stock of the other half-dozen photographs round the room. They established her identity, no more. Fastidiously posed, they were in the style of Academy paintings. Under them you could have written 'Disappointed in Love', 'Thoughts of Last Summer', 'Waiting for a Letter'. They told more about the photographer than his model.

The tall portrait was different. Not relaxed – no studio photograph could be – but not forced either. In this, Cribb sensed instinctively, were genuine indications of character. A distinct misgiving in the eyes, watchful, wanting to trust, but prepared for disappointment. The lips finely shaped, set almost in a pout, sensuous, defiant. A fine balance of confidence and uncertainty, coolness and passion. The hallmarks of murder?

Cribb had come to Park Lodge without making an appointment. He did not propose conducting a conversation through the family solicitor. It was a detached three-storey building on the fashionable north side of Kew Green. He had given his name to a maidservant and she had shown him up to the private part of the house on the top floor. This was a drawing-room, handsomely furnished in rosewood. There was a Steinway grand in the corner.

Mr Cromer, the girl had said, would not be long. He was finishing some work in the studio. Cribb was content to be alone with the picture. From it he derived an impression of Miriam Cromer. A photograph was no substitute for an interview, but it provided contact of a sort, a chance to see her as she had once looked for a few seconds. The camera was objective. If there was much that it could not convey, at least it made an honest statement. *Here is a woman* was what it said, not *Here is a murderess.*

The objectivity ended with the photograph. Cribb used it in a subjective way, beginning by asking himself what could have induced Miriam Cromer to plead guilty to murder. He let the details of that extraordinary confession creep into his mind. He remembered the episode of the improper photographs she had claimed had provoked the blackmail. He could picture her now at twenty, high-spirited, impetuous, taken in by a cheap deception she could not have dreamed would end in murder. He could visualise the outrage in those eyes when Perceval had made his first demand. To be ensnared and physically shamed by a blackmailer could have driven her to devise a way of destroying him.

Her picture made it seem more credible.

What he could not easily accept was the one thing beyond dispute – the fact that she had confessed. She had refused to capitulate to her blackmailer. Why capitulate to justice?

But now the confession was in dispute. She could not have opened the poison cabinet without possessing a key. If what she had confessed was substantially true, why had she not been frank about the key?

There was the possibility that she was trying to save someone else from the gallows. An accomplice. Had she and Howard Cromer plotted the murder together? It was difficult to credit that a man would allow his wife to be hanged while he went free. Did they believe a beautiful woman telling a story of blackmail might earn a reprieve? A reprieve meant penal servitude for life. The silent system. The treadmill. Oakum-picking.

Cribb looked at the slender hands, pale against the dark fabric of the dress.

Was it quite impossible that she was innocent of the crime? Could someone have persuaded or compelled her to make a false confession? That was difficult to credit. The woman in the photograph was not simple-minded. Nor was she timid.

He turned at the approach of footsteps.

Howard Cromer wore a black velvet jacket and red bow-tie. He was pale and deeply lined. His hair was streaked with silver. He spoke breathlessly, from hurrying upstairs. 'My dear sir, I do apologise for keeping you. Once one has started work in the dark-room it is impossible to stop prematurely without damaging the result. Your name, I was advised, is Cribb, but I know nothing else about you.'

'Sergeant Cribb, sir.' He watched the photographer acutely. 'Of the Criminal Investigation Department.'

The brown eyes widened, but the voice betrayed no alarm. 'I confess I thought we had seen the last of you gentlemen at Park Lodge. Are you sent by Inspector Waterlow?'

'In a word, no, sir,' answered Cribb. 'Higher authority, you might say.'

The eyebrows jumped at that. 'Oh. Is that significant?'

'I wouldn't place any significance on it at all if I were you, sir. They like to dot their "i"s and cross their "t"s, that's all. I have been asked to make another check of the statement your wife made. This is the lady, I presume.'

Howard Cromer stepped towards the photograph and stood for a moment staring at it as if he had not seen it before. 'Taken last year, Sergeant, to mark our second wedding anniversary. She is stunningly beautiful, don't you agree?' He took out a handkerchief and touched the corner of one eye with it. In the movement his watch-chain was revealed, an albert, with a small, silver key prominent on it. 'Two and a half years! That is all we have had together. Every minute was precious. To you it may sound odd, Sergeant, coming from a man of my age, but I am enslaved, utterly enslaved. Merely to look at her is the greatest happiness. Even in that ghastly prison one glance at her exquisite face banishes the surroundings for me. Forgive me. I talk incessantly about her.'

'Don't apologise, sir. It's your wife I came to ask you about.'

'Sit down, then.' Cromer showed Cribb to a single-ended sofa and picked up a large volume from a table nearby. 'Look at this. It will speak more objectively than I.' He thrust it into Cribb's hands, a photograph album, morocco with mother-of-pearl inlay. 'It is all here, the story of our life together. All on record. My most precious possession.'

Cribb opened the book. Photograph albums bored him usually. Not this one.

On the first page was a cabinet-sized family portrait: the father, corpulent and bearded, seated beside the mother, an elegant woman in a large hat decorated with flowers; three tall young men behind them; in front, seated on a footstool at her father's feet, Miriam, in a white dress and straw hat; beside her, on the floor, a younger sister.

'The Kilpatrick family complete,' said Howard Cromer. 'One April afternoon in 1885 they came to this house, the seven of them, all the way from Hampstead to sit for a family portrait.'

Cribb made the appropriate comment. 'Your reputation must be widely known, sir.'

Cromer nodded. 'Mr Kilpatrick had seen my work reproduced in *The Tatler* and decided that no other photographer should be engaged. Miriam told me later that she herself drew the

Tatler studies to her father's attention. Poor man, he died six months after this was taken, but I believe the portrait gave him a lot of satisfaction. It's a tolerable result, don't you think? The three at the back are the brothers: William, in the Merchant Taylors' blazer, now in the Indian Civil Service, Gerald, the eldest, back from Canada on a visit, and Edgar, who died of influenza the same year. Dreadful, the ravages of fate. Mrs Kilpatrick passed on last winter.' Sighing, he turned the page. There were two *carte-de-visite* studies of Miriam, one seated. She had the solemn gaze usual in long exposures. 'I took these the following week,' Cromer told Cribb. 'Isn't she sublimely lovely? I was so enchanted with her that I plucked up courage and asked her father if I could take an individual portrait of her.' He smiled. 'That was after I had treated the parents to madeira wine and fruit cake. I said Miriam was a perfect photogenic subject. She blushed to the colour of the madeira and said she would rather not be photographed alone. Her mother told her not to be sensitive and said that if she was photogenic she had a duty to oblige. I remember Mrs Kilpatrick's words: "To Mr Cromer you exist simply as an object to be captured on a photographic plate, like a vase of flowers. I shall not flatter you by discussing the matter any further. Papa will accompany you here next week." The decision was made without her husband uttering a word.'

'The fair sex have a way of settling things among themselves,' Cribb commented. He was thinking such a show of modesty was strange from a young lady who had posed unclothed three years previously, but this was not the moment to mention it.

Cromer turned the page. 'Ah – some of the set I knew before my marriage. The occasion was the fair on Hampstead Heath. Whit Monday, 1885. You can see Miriam in the white Venetian dress. That's Simon Allingham, our solicitor, with his arm round her waist trying to put the photographer off his stroke. I think he succeeded – it is over-exposed, as you can see.' He turned over.

The pictures of Miriam in those few months before her marriage interested Cribb, for they conveyed a sense of gaiety that was absent in the framed portraits round the room. There were picnics, river-outings and tennis afternoons. The same young people appeared in the different settings. Allingham, Cribb noticed, was never far from Miriam. He was easy to spot with his straight fair hair and dazzling smile.

'How long have you know him – young Allingham?'

'Simon? It must be ten years, certainly before he qualified. We hunted together with the Hertfordshire. First-class fellow. A confirmed bachelor. Simon is the only one of this set I have kept up with. He has been a tower of strength these last terrible months.'

Cribb lifted the next page and found that another came with it.

'May I?' said Cromer at once. He took a pen-knife from his pocket. 'If the pages stick, one can do irreparable damage by forcing them.' Sliding the blade between the pages, he found the point and prised them apart. 'There. No harm done, I think. A spot of glue on the mount.'

It had not escaped Cribb that glue on the mount suggested the page had not been opened since the photograph was put in the album. This was odd, considering Howard Cromer had described the album as his most precious possession. Odder still, considering the photograph was of the wedding.

Cromer gave a quick laugh. 'Miriam complains that this is the only photograph I appear in. I arranged for Perceval to take it. As you will have noticed, there's too much of the church wall and not enough of the guests, but it suffices. This was September, 1885. He was fairly new in my employment.'

'September? Your courtship was brief, then?'

'But intensely busy,' said Cromer. 'The pictures you have seen represent only a fraction of the activity. In five months we did enough for three years – theatre, opera, Ascot, Henley and every coming-out party in North London, I think. I was in my fortieth year, you understand. Miriam was only twenty-three. Convention may have called for a longer engagement, but in the circumstances . . .' He held out his hands.

'You were old enough to know your own mind, sir,' Cribb concurred.

'Quite. And Miriam knew hers,' Cromer emphasised, 'else I might have hesitated. I was enraptured with her from the beginning – what man with a sense of beauty would not be? – but I needed to be reassured that I would be an acceptable husband. She convinced me that I was the only man alive that she would consider marrying. That was music to my ears – to know that I might see her marvellous face each day of my life, in countless places, by daylight, gas-light, moonlight, discovering new aspects of her beauty. It was all I could desire. It made a young man of me. I don't look too bad in my morning suit, do I?'

'I wouldn't put you at forty, sir.'

'Decent of you to say so. There's Simon, my best man. Doesn't Miriam look stunning? The dress was by Pingat, in percale, with ecru lace and real pearl buttons. Her father was a wealthy man, a former mayor of Hampstead. He provided a magnificent reception and paid for the honeymoon as well. Fifteen days in Trouville.' He turned the pages more swiftly. 'I took my Rouch Eureka hand camera. The definition is not so good as I hoped for. There's Miriam promenading. The races at Deauville. Outside the Casino. We played *chemin-de-fer* until it closed most evenings. There's Miriam on a wagonette.'

Cribb stopped the page with his finger. It was the first picture in the album with the wistful look he had noticed in the framed portrait. He passed no comment, letting the pages run on. The outdoor pictures gave way to studio portraits of Miriam, always in different clothes.

'Your wife is well provided with gowns, sir.'

'She lacks nothing,' said Cromer matter-offactly. 'It is my custom to give her the material things the fair sex take pleasure in.' He chuckled. 'After all, each new gown is an occasion for another portrait, as you will have observed. The accessories too, the fans and hats and jewellery, are continuously replaced. It is a trivial amusement of mine to surprise her by leaving small presents about the house in places where I know she will accidentally find them. A box of chocolates, a mother-of-pearl brooch, a silver charm.'

Cribb felt a comment was in order but could not supply one. His prosaic style of speech was not equipped for this. The words gushed from Cromer as liberally as his self-attested kindnesses to Miriam. It would have been interesting to have known what her response had been. If the photographs were any indication, it was not wholly favourable.

'She is my inspiration,' Cromer went on. 'All my best work is here. Some of it I have enlarged and put in my bedroom, it delights me so. I take a section of a photograph and enlarge it to life size. As a matter of fact, I was making a print of her hands when you arrived. I find it occupies my mind to work. Private work, I must emphasise. I have refused all commissions since the tragedy happened.'

'This unfortunate event must have hit your business hard,' Cribb observed.

A sigh. 'I fear so. For the present, I am not short of funds. There was a substantial legacy when Miriam's father died which we have not touched.'

If she had not pleaded guilty, Cribb reflected,

counsel for the defence might have taken a slice of that in fees. 'I heard that you built your business up by your own efforts, sir.'

'That's absolutely true.' A faint look of self-congratulation passed across Cromer's features. 'I am a self-made man. This studio has a reputation second to none on this side of London, or had, until this happened. Without exaggeration, I could show you portraits enough of the nobility to illustrate *Debrett*. I was planning a second studio in Regent Street.'

'But you won't give up the trade?'

Cromer looked injured. '*Trade* isn't the expression I would use. No, this is my art, and I shall continue to practise it. In twenty-two years I have come a long way in photography. When I began in the sixties, it was the peak of the *carte* mania. Every gentleman insisted on being posed leaning on a cardboard column, top hat in hand and one leg crossed over the other – an excruciating pose to hold for a thirty-second exposure, as the strained attitudes showed. If anything, the experience was worse for the photographer, who had the job of explaining to the sitter that an iron head-rest would be necessary to fix the pose, that red hair would come out black so he would have to be puffed, and that a plate was ruined because he had blinked. I have often said I would sooner be the public hangman.'

Cribb let the remark pass. It had slipped off Cromer's tongue as carelessly as his own reference to trade. 'Have you always lived in Kew, sir?'

'Four years only. My studio here represents many years of tiresome work photographing vicious little boys in sailor suits.' He gave a cheerless laugh. 'You would not believe the number of spoilt plates I have sold to glass merchants at a few shillings a ton because of small heads that turned just as I removed the lens cap. At one time I worked from a wooden shed on the promenade at Worthing, but that is in confidence, Sergeant. I would not wish any of my present clients to know of it. I moved about the suburbs a good deal earlier in my career. Bethnal Green, Tooting Bec, Cricklewood – the localities improved with my fortune.'

'I don't suppose you could afford to employ an assistant in the early days.'

'Good Lord, no. I was on my own for years. I prepared my own paper, sensitised the plates, acted as receptionist, photographer, developer, printer, retoucher and clerk.'

'It's a wonder you had time to sleep, sir.'

Cromer grinned. 'Sleep is not so important when you are young. Eating was more of a problem. I lived on egg-yolks. It takes a devil of a lot of egg-white to albumenise a ream of paper.'

'Was Josiah Perceval your first assistant, sir?'

'The second, actually. The first, certainly, with any photographic knowledge. He was a local man, living in Sheen. I took him on soon after I moved here. The worst mistake of my life.' Howard Cromer closed the album and gripped it to his chest. 'The man was a viper, Sergeant, and I failed to see it. As an assistant he seemed to be competent, reasonably conscientious, good with clients. He was uppish at times, I admit. I knew he helped himself to wine, for instance, and I think he used my stationery for personal correspondence. I ought to have checked him at the outset. I was too indulgent by far. I look for the merits in people and ignore their faults. It was quite beyond imagination that he could be persecuting Miriam. If I had got the smallest suspicion . . .' He shook his head slowly. 'She, poor innocent, suffered alone. She said not a word about him, Sergeant, not one word.'

'Why was that, sir?'

Cromer drew a deep breath. 'That is something I have asked myself repeatedly. I have to admit that I failed her. She was afraid to confide in me. My own beloved wife!' His knuckles whitened with the force of his grip on the album. 'Those words in her confession are seared across my soul. *To confide in my husband was no solution.* She was unable to turn to me in her torment.'

'There are secrets in most marriages,' Cribb ventured. He had some sympathy for Miriam Cromer. She was more real to this man as a series of photographs than a wife.

'She was just a child. What secrets could she have had?' said Cromer more to himself than Cribb. 'I take all the responsibility for what happened. Mine is an excitable temperament, and Miriam was terrified how I would react if I knew that Perceval had the means to destroy my reputation, my livelihood. It was easier for her to pay him than confide in me. And when his demands became intolerable she tried to resolve the problem in her own way, poor child.'

Cribb glanced at the picture on the wall. They were not the eyes of a child.

'I can't believe she was frightened of you, sir. From what you tell me, you never gave her cause for fear.'

'Good Lord, no! I have never uttered a word in anger to Miriam.'

'There were no misunderstandings between you? It's not uncommon in the first year or two of marriage.'

'Misunderstandings?' Cromer repeated, and thought a moment. 'Nothing of any consequence. It is fair to say that she had some difficulty in adjusting to the marriage bond, but that was in the first six months or so, and it was my fault, mine entirely. I lacked imagination. I should have seen what a change her life had undergone. For months we had led an extremely active social life, as I told you a moment ago. We moved in a spirited set of young people, doing everything in the social calendar, and more. After our marriage I wanted Miriam to myself. To see her in my own home, talk to her, photograph her was all I desired. I tried to make this house sufficient for all our needs. What I failed to anticipate was that when I was working, as I was obliged to, she became bored. I engaged a companion for her, Miss Poley, a personable lady in her sixties, proficient at needlework, music and many card games, but in a short time Miriam asked me to dismiss her. With reluctance, I agreed. It was not the answer. We tried to find things Miriam could do in the house without usurping the housekeeper. She agreed to arrange the flowers in the studio and fill the decanters – things a lady could legitimately undertake – but there were still hours when she was unoccupied. She started taking solitary walks in Kew Gardens. I was reluctant – the classic example of a middle-aged husband fearful of losing his pretty young wife – but I gave my consent, and she seemed happier as a result. It appears so trivial now!'

'You gave up your former friends completely after your marriage, did you, sir?'

'All except Simon. He still came to dinner once a fortnight. To be candid, I was worried Miriam might weary of me and find the younger people more amusing. I am a jealous and possessive man and that is the truth.'

'But you trusted your wife?'

'She was a child,' Cromer said again.

'Her innocence was precious to you?'

'Supremely.'

Cribb gave a nod. It was not for him to lecture Howard Cromer on the practicalities of marriage, but he understood the vulnerability in the young wife's eyes. And he could see why she had found it impossible to confide her secret.

'Nothing that has happened has shaken my devotion to her,' Cromer went on. 'To lose her, Sergeant, will be . . .' He stopped, unable to face the possibility. 'Is there a chance, do you think, that . . . ?'

Cribb shook his head. 'I couldn't say what is in the Home Secretary's mind, sir. If it isn't too distressing, I should like to take a look at the studio.'

Cromer got up at once. 'I am absolutely at your disposal. It is on the ground floor.'

As they made their way down a carpeted staircase, Cribb asked, 'Where were you on the day Perceval died, sir?'

Cromer gave him a sharp glance. 'In Brighton, Sergeant. The Portrait Photographers' League was holding its annual conference. I am Vice-Chairman.'

'Of course. Should have remembered. I read it in the statement your wife made.' Cribb paused to look out of a window. 'What time did you leave the house that day, sir?'

'Early,' answered Cromer. 'I cannot be exact as to the time.'

'You were catching a particular train?'

'No particular one. The Brighton service is frequent, as you must know.'

'What time did the conference begin, sir?'

'At eleven, Sergeant.'

'Then you must have started early. It would take the best part of two hours to get to Brighton from here. You were there in time, I hope?'

'The trains are most reliable,' Cromer answered, pushing open a door. 'This is the reception room. The entire ground floor suite has been converted into studio accommodation.'

Cribb stepped inside, expecting a row of chairs and a pile of magazines. He swiftly learned not to confuse photography with dentistry or men's haircutting. This was no common waiting-room. It was high and spacious, with a pink and white wall-covering that looked like brocade. The design was repeated in pale blue and yellow in the fabric covers of a carved gilt sofa and chairs in the Louis XIV style. The opulence extended to twin cut-glass chandeliers, an ebonised occasional table and a display cabinet crowded with fine porcelain. Round the walls were ranged framed photographs of purposeful-looking men in frock coats standing beside tall-backed chairs as if they had just risen to make statements of surpassing interest.

'The doors to right and left lead to the dressing-rooms,' Cromer explained. 'The ladies in particular use the powder-puff up to the last possible moment, while no gentleman will submit himself to the lens without straightening his tie.' He pushed open a pair of doors flanked by tall vases of pampas grass and announced, 'My studio, Sergeant.'

It was as large as the booking-hall at Kew Gardens station. What had once been a spacious drawing room had been more than doubled in size by removing the north-facing wall and extending the room outwards into the garden. Besides giving additional space, the extension was obviously designed to admit as much natural light as possible. It was formed largely of glass and dominated by a broad skylight that could be blocked out by a blind operated with pulleys and a cord.

'Fit for the Queen herself!' ejaculated Cribb. He strode to the centre to examine a camera large enough to seat a cabman. Ahead was the podium where clients could be posed in suitable attitudes among profile props that included a stile, a church steeple and a rowing-boat. 'I'm no authority on photography,' he said conversationally, 'but I don't under-estimate its possibilities. We photograph habitual criminals to assist us in detecting crime, did you know that? Half-profile, to get the shape of the nose, you understand, and in their own clothes, naturally. I don't suggest the results could be compared with yours. We don't take much trouble over posing the sitters, and retouching isn't included, but the character comes through. There's no artistry in it, of course,' he tactfully added.

Cromer had already moved through the room to another door. He seemed keen to make the tour as quick as possible.

'That cabinet to your left,' said Cribb. 'Would that by any chance be where the wine is kept? I see you have some glasses on the top.'

'I do beg your pardon,' said Cromer, in a fluster. 'Do have a drink.' He started towards the mahogany chiffonier Cribb had indicated. 'Will it be sherry or madeira?'

Cribb's hand shot up to refuse. 'Thank you, but not on duty, sir. But I would like to see inside if I may.'

Cromer took a key from his pocket, unlocked one of the doors and showed Cribb two cut-glass decanters. 'The one containing poison is still in the hands of the police,' he said. 'I was told I shall get it back eventually.'

'Are the decanters always kept locked in here, sir?'

'Oh no. When clients come, I have them on top, to offer them a glass. It helps to put them at their ease. Photography is an awesome experience to the uninitiated, Sergeant.'

'But you lock the decanters in here when you are not expecting clients?'

'That is correct. I do not believe in putting temptation in people's way.'

'Servants, you mean?'

Cromer nodded. 'Although when it came to secret drinking, I was perfectly sure that my assistant was the principal culprit. He was partial to madeira and it was quite obvious that the level went down each time I left him to work alone in the studio.'

'He had a key, then?'

'He had to have one, because there were times when he took charge of sittings,' Cromer said.

'I see. And your wife filled the decanters once a week on Mondays. How much goes into one of these, sir? A bottle and a half?'

'Almost as much as that.'

'That's a lot of wine in a week.'

'I have a lot of clients.'

'But on the day Perceval died, you had no appointments. Is that right?'

'Yes. I was going to Brighton. There was plenty of retouching and mounting for Perceval to do, so I kept the day free of sittings.'

'And that was why the decanters were inside this chiffonier and not on top?'

'Obviously.'

'But you were pretty sure Perceval would help himself to some during the day?'

'It was more likely than not,' said Cromer. 'Perhaps you would care to see the other rooms now?' He opened a door from which a smell of ether came. 'The processing room. I was working here this morning, so I must ask you to forgive the mess.'

It was a long room with a table in the centre, a desk and a number of cupboards. There was a lead sink in the corner.

'So this is where he died?'

Cromer waved his hand vaguely over a section of the carpeted floor. 'He was lying here when the servants came in. The chair was on its side by the desk there, and the wine glass had fallen near it.' He moistened his lips and took a nervous step back as Cribb moved towards the desk.

'The kitchen is underneath us, I take it,' said Cribb.

'It is.' Cromer frowned. 'How did you know?'

'The plumbing. Which one is the poison cabinet, sir?'

Cromer moved his right forefinger in the direction to Cribb's left. Cribb went over to the cabinet, which was white like the other cupboards in the room, and tapped it with his knuckle. 'Sounds solid. Could I see inside, sir?'

'The cyanide was removed.'

'I'd still like to look inside.'

Cromer fumbled with the front of his waistcoat.

'That's a capital idea, sir, having the key on your watch-chain,' Cribb commented. 'No risk of leaving it about the place.' He watched Cromer fit the key into the lock. 'It looks a strong lock, too. May I?'

With a shrug, Cromer detached the watch-chain from his waistcoat and stepped aside.

Cribb turned the key. He could tell by the snugness of the fit that it was not the sort of lock you could open in five minutes with a bent hatpin.

There were perhaps a dozen bottles inside. Cribb gave them a glance, withdrew the key and pushed the door shut. 'Ah. It locks automatically.'

'It is of German manufacture,' Cromer explained. 'I had it specially imported from Lubeck when I moved here.'

'That must have put you to some expense, sir.'

'Where poison is concerned, one has an obligation to take every possible precaution against an accident,' said Cromer. 'Of one thing I can assure you: there was no negligence in the tragedy that happened here. We were all aware of the lethal effect of potassium cyanide.'

'What is its purpose in photography, sir?'

'We used it a lot more in the wet collodion process than we do now that we work with dry plates. It was then used mainly as a fixing agent, but I still find it indispensable for reducing the density of negatives. Believe me, we are mindful of its dangers. Even the fumes can kill, Sergeant.

We always ensure that the room is adequately ventilated when we work with it.'

Cribb tried the lock again. 'There are just two keys to this cabinet, yours and Perceval's — is that correct, sir?'

'Yes,' Cromer responded in a way that partially anticipated the next question.

'On the day Perceval was murdered, you were in Brighton. Where was your key?'

Cromer put his hand to the front of his waistcoat and groped for the absent watch-chain. His eyes widened momentarily.

Cribb held it out to him. 'Thank you, sir.'

'On the day Perceval died, it never left my person,' said Cromer as he fixed it in place again. 'Is there some difficulty over the key?'

The question was couched just a shade too casually. 'No,' said Cribb in an even voice, 'no difficulty that I can think of.' He picked up a print from the table, glanced at the picture and turned it over. In the centre of an intricate design of loops and curlicues, between two trumpeting angels, were the words *Howard Cromer, Photographic Artist, The Green, Kew.* 'Do you know what I should like to borrow if you have such a thing? A photograph of your wife.'

Cromer's face relaxed. 'You shall have one with my compliments. There is no shortage here of portraits of Miriam.'

'That's good,' said Cribb. 'The one I want, if you have it in a size convenient for my pocket, is that one upstairs in the drawing room. The one I was looking at when you came in.'

Just after seven, the postman came.

Berry was shaving.

'Two,' his wife called up. 'From London.'

'Put 'em on t'shelf, then.'

'Aren't you going to open them?'

'In good time, woman. I'm busy just now.'

When he came downstairs his eggs and bacon were ready. Nothing ever came between Berry and breakfast. While he was eating, his wife took the letters off the shelf, had another look at the handwriting and placed them on the table by his plate.

One he saw at a glance was from the Sheriff of London. He had got to know the brown envelope with the crest on the flap. There was no reason to open it yet. It was a job, and he knew which one.

The other interested him more. A white envelope. Copperplate. Since taking up his present office he had received a fair number of letters, most of them from crackpots. He had learned to recognise them by the way they addressed the envelope – *James Berry, Hangman, Yorkshire* – something after that style, and spelt wrong as often as not. It was a wonder they reached him. The Post Office did a grand job. He burned them mostly.

'Do I get tea this morning, or not?'

As soon as his wife went into the scullery, he opened the white envelope. It was from Madame Tussaud's. He had never been so surprised in his life. The letter he had spent most of last week putting together was still in his pocket. He felt to make sure. Took it out and checked the writing on the envelope. He had decided not to post it until the Newgate job was confirmed. He put it back. He would not need to send it now.

They wanted to make a waxwork of him.

'No doubt you are aware,' their letter stated, 'that your predecessor in the office of executioner, the late Mr Marwood, permitted us the privilege of modelling his portrait from life on more than one occasion. The figure was an object of unfailing interest to our patrons, among whom we have been honoured to welcome the members of our own Royal Family and the Sovereigns and Rulers of many nations of the world. We would deem it a privilege if you would consent to sit for us and permit us to include your likeness in the Exhibition.

'Should you contemplate a visit to London in the weeks to come, we would be honoured to arrange for you to visit the Exhibition. If you should consent to sit for your portrait, an appointment could be made at any time convenient to yourself. Be assured that in the presentation of its exhibits Madame Tussaud's has ever observed the highest standards of good taste.'

That was clear from their letter. Beautifully turned phrases. Not a hint that old Marwood was down in the Chamber of Horrors with Burke and Hare and Charlie Peace and the wickedest villains in the annals of crime. Not that Berry objected to that. When you had put

106

the straps on a few and seen them off, it was no disgrace to stand beside them in a waxwork show. From what he remembered of his only visit to Tussaud's they stood the murderers in rows in a representation of the dock. Marwood's figure was quite separate, facing them, his pinioning-strap at the ready. *An object of unfailing interest to our patrons.*

Before his wife came back with the tea he slipped his letter out of sight, behind the frame containing his murderers in the front room. It was the one place where she would never look.

He went back to finish breakfast. The brown envelope from the Sheriff of London was still there on the table. In the excitement he had clean forgotten it.

'Look alive, Cromer!'

Prison Officer Bell watched as the condemned woman removed the handkerchief from her eyes and turned her head. The fine hair strewn across the grey calico sheet shimmered with the movement.

'You have to see the governor. Nine sharp.'

'The governor has asked to see me?' She made it sound like an invitation to dinner.

'Isn't that what I said? On your feet, now. I want you washed, dressed and fed, your cell scrubbed and your bedding tidied first.'

Without another word the prisoner obeyed. To Bell's way of thinking, it was unnatural, the way she acted, as if she was indifferent to Newgate. It was impossible to dredge up sympathy for her. She had not shed a tear since the day she came in, nor looked to the wardresses for comfort. Bell could be generous with comfort if it was appreciated. She could talk anyone round to a happier frame of mind. There was no call for comfort from this one.

The wardresses had discussed it in their room. Hawkins had said it was good breeding, that a lady was trained to bottle up her feelings. To that, Bell had said she always understood ladies were taught to make conversation. 'Not to the likes of us,' Hawkins had replied. That had rankled with Bell. What business had a common murderess acting as if she was superior to them? Cromer was a cold-blooded killer and the story that her victim had been blackmailing her made no difference. It made it worse, in Bell's view, for what was the cause of the blackmail? Lewd photographs. 'If that's a lady,' she told Hawkins, 'show me a whore.'

At a quarter to nine they escorted her through the ill-lit passages to the governor's room. They stood by the door waiting for the bell of St Sepulchre to strike the hour.

In spite of herself, Bell started whispering words of comfort. 'The governor ain't such a hard man really. We've seen a lot of him, Hawkins and me. He's one of Nature's gentlemen.'

'A trump,' Hawkins concurred.

They need not have troubled. Cromer gave no sign that she had heard one word. Yet she was not completely oblivious to what was going on. At the first stroke of nine, she gave a small shudder of tension.

Hawkins knocked.

In greeting the prisoner, the governor called her *Mrs* Cromer. 'You may step forward.'

He had a piece of paper in his hand.

'You are sleeping better now, I hope?' he said. 'How long is it that you have been in Newgate?'

In a clear voice she answered, 'Ten days since the trial, sir.'

'Ten days,' he repeated absently. He looked down at the paper. 'I asked to see you because I have received a communication concerning you.'

Bell noticed the prisoner's hands clench suddenly.

The governor continued, 'You will remember that when I spoke to you in this room on your first day here I cautioned you to reconcile yourself to the sentence of the law. You have tried to follow that advice, I trust?'

'Yes, sir.' There was a note of expectation in her voice, as if she could not wait for him to come to the point.

'This is from the Sheriff of the City of London. It is the warrant for your execution. It will take place a week from today at eight in the morning.'

How gently spoken, Bell thought. He might have been telling her he had tickets for the Lyceum.

The prisoner stood numbly. For an instant Bell thought she was going to sway.

'Do you wish to sit down?' the governor asked her.

A shake of the head.

'It is simply a stage in the legal procedure,'

he went on. 'So far as you are concerned, it will mean that you return now to a different part of the prison, a different cell. The same officers will be in attendance. You may exercise when you wish, accompanied by them. And you may receive visitors in the cell – your husband, and your solicitor, if you wish. The regulations forbid you from receiving any form of gift from them, or from physical contact. Do you understand?'

She was standing still with her eyes closed.

'Did you hear what I said, Mrs Cromer?'

She nodded.

'I shall continue to visit you each day and you may speak to me or the chaplain if anything troubles you. I urge you again to commend your soul to the Almighty. He receives those who repent their sins.' He signalled to the wardresses.

They stepped forward, gripped her firmly by the arms and guided her out.

As they walked, Bell was tempted to tell the prisoner that if she had been willing to confide in those who knew about prison routine, they could have spared her some of the pain of that experience, but she checked herself. Words would be wasted on this one. Better to see what difference the condemned cell made to Mrs Miriam Cromer.

'Upstairs here.'

They mounted one of Newgate's iron staircases, Bell leading to unlock the door of the condemned block. 'This way, your ladyship. If you take a look through here' – they had stopped by a window too narrow even to be fitted with bars – 'you can see the exercise yard.'

The prisoner glanced down at a small, cobbled square in deep shadow.

'That's yours. Exclusive,' Bell told her. 'We're supposed to take you down there for a constitutional any time you feel inclined. It ain't Hyde Park exactly, but it's a place to go, ain't it?'

The prisoner looked away.

'Don't you like it?' Bell asked. 'I suppose you can't wait to see your new home. Come on, then.'

They passed two open cell doors and entered the next.

It was limewashed and lit by a gaslamp covered with a bright tin shade. There was a table with three wooden stools ranged round it. To the right was a narrow iron bedstead with a flock mattress and blankets folded on top. On a shelf built across one corner were a copper basin, some eating utensils and a Bible. A tap protruded from the corner opposite. Under it was the latrine-bucket.

Hawkins closed the door. The sound echoed through the building.

The wardresses watched the prisoner, waiting for a reaction. Sometimes they screamed so much that the doctor had to be called to them.

'This is larger than the other cell.'

'It needs to be, for three and a visitor sometimes,' said Bell, pulling out a stool for herself. 'We still have to watch you by turns, two at a time, day and night. It's no different in the c.c., you know.'

'What is that – c.c.?'

Hawkins chose that moment to make one of her rare utterances. 'Do you play cards, Cromer? We're allowed to play cards with you. Bell and me know just about all the three-handed games you ever heard of. Nap, rummy, poker, cribbage. Cards is a wonderful way of passing the time.'

'No thank you.' The prisoner turned to Bell. 'You didn't answer my question, miss.'

Damned impertinence! When she said it, that 'miss' never sounded like a term of respect. Bell took a pack of playing cards from her pocket and shuffled them. 'If you really want to know, it's the name we give the cell. "C" for cell, follow me? The first "c" could stand for cards, couldn't it? But seeing as you don't feel disposed to play cards, how would you care for a game of draughts instead? Then we can call it the d.c. What about that, eh?' She rocked with laughter.

Cribb had spent Monday footing it round
Brentford and Kew checking the statements in
the file at Scotland Yard – work for a constable.
As there was no constable assigned to the case,
he had done it himself. It was a self-inflicted
chore. He was unwilling to rely on any statement taken by Inspector Waterlow. So he had
talked to the Brentford pawnbroker Miriam
Cromer had done business with, he had seen
Dr Eagle in his surgery and he had spent two
hours questioning the servants at Park Lodge.
Nothing significant had emerged. It was dis-
piriting to admit, but he could not fault Waterlow's work.

Over a solitary beer that evening he had concluded that whatever the outcome of this inquiry, there was nothing in it for him. If he
proved beyond doubt that Miriam Cromer had
made a false confession and been convicted of
a crime she did not commit, the embarrassment
to the judiciary, the Home Office, the police
did not bear thinking about. The hullabaloo
would be heard all over England. Nobody
would thank him. And if his inquiry upheld
the verdict of the court, it would simply under-
line the thoroughness of Waterlow's work. In
handing on this case, Chief Inspector Jowett
had played his meanest trick.

Tuesday morning found him in the Strand,
at the office of the Portrait Photographers'
League. He had decided to make an indepen-

dent check of Howard Cromer's movements on the day of the murder.

The League shared the second floor with an insurance broker. Cribb's knock was answered by a worried-looking clerk in a thin suit of faded black and a frayed collar.

'Yes?'

'This *is* the Portrait Photographers' League?'

'Yes.'

'Excellent. And who are you?'

'Wallis, sir. The clerk.'

'Well, Wallis, may I come in?'

'But I don't know – '

'A member,' Cribb said with plausible stiffness. 'There is no objection, I trust, to a member calling?'

'This is only the office,' Wallis said, keeping a firm hold on the door. 'Members generally meet at the Burlington Fine Arts Club, to which the League is affiliated. That is in Savile Row.'

'That's no good to me,' said Cribb. 'You are the man who can help me. You *do* have the minutes of the Annual General Meeting here?'

'Somewhere, but I am not certain – '

'Then kindly produce them, would you? I don't have a lot of time.'

The clerk took a deep breath and said, 'That really isn't possible this morning.'

'Not possible?' said Cribb in a shocked voice. 'Not possible for a member to inspect the minutes of the A.G.M.? Are you familiar with the Constitution?'

A moment later he was in the office with a copy of the minutes in his hand.

A theory he had gently nurtured for two days took a turn for the worse as he read, '*The Annual General Meeting at the Metropole Hotel, Brighton, 12th March, 1888. Owing to the indisposition of the Chairman, the Vice-Chairman presided. Opening the meeting, he welcomed the sixty-three members present.*'

He asked Wallis, 'Were you at Brighton this year?'

'I was, sir.'

'It says here that the Vice-Chairman presided. That is correct?'

'Quite correct, sir.'

'The meeting opened in the morning, I believe. There was no delay?'

'No delay, sir. It started sharp at eleven.'

If Howard Cromer had opened the A.G.M. at eleven, he must have left Kew soon after nine that morning.

'How long did it go on?'

'It should tell you in the minutes, sir. Some time after four, as I recollect. There was an adjournment for lunch, of course. That was between one o'clock and half past two.'

'Mr Cromer presided for the whole of the meeting, did he?'

Wallis frowned. 'Mr Cromer, sir?'

'Howard Cromer – the Vice-Chairman.'

'No, sir. Mr Cromer did not take the chair.'

Cribb held out the minutes. 'This states quite clearly that the Vice-Chairman presided Mr Cromer is the Vice-Chairman, is he not?'

'He is, to be sure,' said the clerk, 'but at the start of the A.G.M. he was not. If you recall the agenda, sir, one of the final items of business was the election of the new committee. Mr Cromer is the *new* Vice-Chairman. Mr Darting-ton-Fisher, of the outgoing committee, presided. The new committee were elected towards the end of the afternoon.'

Cribb's eye raced down the minutes. *'Election of Committee for 1888/9. Messrs. D. C. Turner (Chairman), H. Cromer (Vice-Chairman) and W. Hollinghurst (Secretary) were elected unopposed. Mr J. Templeton and Mr P. Hartley-Smith were nominated for the position of Treasurer, Mr Templeton being elected by forty-seven votes to thirty-one.'*

So Howard Cromer had been in Brighton on the afternoon of the murder – or had he?

'These nominations: were they made in advance of the meeting?'

'Naturally, sir. If you recall the Constitution – '

'Were these gentleman present at the meeting?'

'Assuredly,' said Wallis, toppling Cribb's theory with a word.

'You're positive?'

'If it is Mr Cromer you are thinking of, I spoke to him myself at the conclusion of the meeting, sir.'

With a click of the tongue, Cribb resumed his reading of the minutes. He wanted to see if there was any evidence that Cromer had been present at Brighton in the morning.

'Here's a queer thing,' he presently said. 'The Treasurer was elected by forty-seven votes to thirty-one. Would you check my mental arithmetic, Wallis? Forty-seven and thirty-one comes to more than sixty-three, doesn't it? It states at the beginning that there were sixty-three members in attendance at this A.G.M.'

'Sixty-three in the morning, sir. A number of members were unable to be present for that session from pressure of business. The election is generally held over until the afternoon to ensure that members arriving late have an opportunity to register their votes.'

Possibilities mounting again, Cribb asked, 'You wouldn't recollect who arrived late?'

Wallis shook his head. 'My memory doesn't go back to March, sir. Not unless' – he reached for a box-file – 'they wrote to the secretary advising him that they were unable to be present in the morning.'

Cribb waited while the clerk sorted through the contents of the file.

'A lot of these are simple apologies for absence. I dare say you sent one yourself, sir. Now here are some pinned together. These, I think –'

'May I?' Cribb whipped the small sheaf of letters out of the clerk's hand and riffled through them. 'Ah.'

The first piece of new evidence to come his way. On headed notepaper from Park Lodge, dated Sunday, 11th March, 1888, Howard Cromer had written:

My dear Thorne,

This is to advise you that I am unfortunately prevented by another commitment from

attending the first session of the A.G.M. to-
morrow. In tendering my apology, I assure you
that I shall be present after lunch and that I
wish my nomination for the Committee to
stand.

> *Sincerely,*
> *H. Cromer'*

'You won't need this,' said Cribb, pocketing
it. The others he handed back.

'Just a moment, sir!'

'Regrettably,' said Cribb, 'I haven't another
moment to spare. Good day to you, Wallis.'

Out in the Strand, he started whistling.
This was a thankless assignment, but it was
still pleasing to have picked up something
Waterlow had missed. As he approached the
Proud Peacock, he decided to treat himself to
a pint of his favourite brew.

Alone at a table under the window, he took
out the letter and read it again. He was entitled
to feel elated. It was a development.

*. . . I am unfortunately prevented by another
commitment . . .* There was no mention on the
file at Scotland Yard of Howard Cromer having
another commitment. The information did not
incriminate him, but it destroyed the alibi
everyone had assumed he possessed. He had not
been in Brighton on the morning of the murder. That innocent-sounding expression
'another commitment' could have a sinister
meaning.

Cribb saw no difficulty in casting Howard
Cromer in the role of murderer. The motive
Miriam had supplied would serve equally well

for him. If she had decided, after all, to confide in him, tell him Perceval had been black-mailing her for months, he might well have resorted to murder. Anyone threatening to blight Cromer's career with scandal about his wife was touching him on the raw. Ambition and blind devotion made a dangerous combination. In Cribb's judgment, Cromer was a man capable of resolving the problem ruthlessly.

If he had committed murder and it had been discovered, it was possible that Miriam, blaming herself for what had happened, had agreed to make a false confession.

It was time he tested the truth of that story of blackmail, of innocent young ladies duped into displaying their bodies for improper photographs. It was no secret to the police or anyone else that the trade in such things was centred in Holywell Street, five minutes from where he was sitting. Some half-dozen shops purveyed what they euphemistically termed 'art studies'. They were patronised by errant schoolboys, provincials, gentlemen who should know better and Inspector Moser of Scotland Yard, whose purifying zeal was periodically praised by the Bow Street Magistrates.

Miriam Cromer had named Holywell Street in her confession, but Cribb attached small importance to that. The information, if it was to be believed at all, came from Perceval, who was unlikely to have divulged his real source to his victim. Most probably he had mentioned Holywell Street to alarm her. The knowledge that her picture was on open sale in that quarter would be sufficient to secure any respectable woman's co-operation. Still, it had to be investigated.

It was a slum of a street, due for demolition in the proposed improvements to the Strand. One glance along the narrow pavement cluttered with trestle tables surrounded by silent groups of men was sufficient to discourage all but the most determined. In fact not all the trade was pernicious. A jeweller's and two tobacconists' provided pretexts for the not so bold to venture there.

Cribb sifted patiently through a tray of photographs of music hall performers until the question he expected was asked: 'Were you looking for anything in particular, sir?'

He glanced round at the proprietor, a mid-European by his accent, shabby, in carpet slippers and wearing pebble glasses. 'Yes, these are not exactly to my taste. Artistic subjects interest me more. Do you have anything after the style of Lord Leighton?'

'Lord Leighton. I think I know what you mean, sir. Something illustrative of the classic myths, eh? If you would care to step inside . . .'

The tray he was shown contained about sixty faded photographs of women so well concealed in gauze that they would not have looked out of place at the Lord Mayor's Banquet. In the next twenty minutes he graduated by trays to what were labelled *poses plastiques*, arrangements of listless models in thick fleshings.

'You have nothing more' – he turned his

eyes towards the inner part of the shop – 'artistic than these?'

The proprietor shook his head. 'Not at present, sir. I may, of course, get some. If you could come back on another occasion . . .'

This required a different approach. By conventional methods it would take a week to win the confidence of Holywell Street.

Farther up was a shop sporting a green awning with the words *Gallery of Fine Art – J. Brodski (prop.)* Cribb marched straight in and found J. Brodski.

'Where can we talk in confidence?'

He was shown to an office at the back. It contained a desk heaped with old newspapers and unwashed crockery. There was a smell of stale cigar smoke.

Brodski looked anxious, a fat, bearded man with restless eyes and bad teeth.

'You know who I am?' barked Cribb.

Brodski whispered, 'Police?'

Cribb flourished his identification.

'Mr Moser he was here last month,' protested Brodski in a voice of alarm. 'So help me, it is true. My case it came up at Bow Street Friday. I was fined twenty-five pounds.'

'Twenty-five pounds!' Cribb started to laugh.

'Please tell me what is funny about that.'

Cribb let him flounder a little. 'You say you were fined twenty-five pounds!'

The sweat was beading on Brodski's forehead.

'I don't deal in *misdemeanours*,' Cribb went on, articulating the word with contempt. 'Do you think it interests me what smutty little

121

pictures you keep locked in the drawer of this desk? You could have the Queen herself mother-naked on a tigerskin rug. I don't care a twopenny damn. The crime I'm investigating will get you put away for life, Brodski. That's if your life is spared.'

Brodski had turned the colour of the awning outside his shop. 'Please, I do not understand,' he said in a strangled voice.

'Of course you understand,' said Cribb, tight-lipped. 'There's a man dead, Brodski. Murdered. He came here last winter to buy pictures of this woman.' He took out the photograph of Miriam Cromer and pushed it across the desk.

'Straight, I never see this lady in my life!' squeaked Brodski. 'God strike me down, I know nothing of this thing.'

'You're lying!' said Cribb in a snarl. 'He bought some pictures, three or four at least, one called *Aphrodite with Handmaidens*. He came back in March and asked to buy the plates.'

'No, no! I swear it – I never sell such picture. You make the mistake, please believe me.'

Cribb sat grim-faced through the histrionics.

'You don't believe?' finished Brodski.

'Not a word.'

The fat man pitched into another crescendo. 'This not the only picture shop in Holywell Street. There is four, five others. Maybe this man go there. You think?'

Cribb shook his head.

'What will happen?' asked Brodski in despair. 'What you do with me now?'

'Find me an envelope. A clean one.'

Brodski unlocked the desk and rummaged through the drawer, in his confusion uncovering prints enough to put him away for months.

Cribb addressed the envelope to himself at Scotland Yard. 'I'm giving you one chance, Brodski. We know that a shopkeeper in Holywell Street sold pictures of this woman to the man who was murdered. I shan't ask you to peach on one of your neighbours. It doesn't interest me who handled the photographs. What I want from you is the name and address of the supplier — the man who printed the photographs and owns the negatives. You understand? Take this picture, show it to the others in the street, get that information and write it on the back.' He took out his watch and flicked up the lid. 'It's almost half past two. That gives you three and a half hours. Put the photograph in the envelope and see that it catches the six o'clock post at Charing Cross. It will reach me at Scotland Yard by the last delivery, at eight tonight. If it doesn't come, Brodski, you can expect me here within the hour. It won't be twenty-five pounds this time.'

The letter reached the Yard by the 8 p.m. delivery. Cribb had sorted through the post before the duty constable knew it had arrived. Such eagerness was exceptional. In the regular way he would have left the thing unopened till next morning. This was not a regular investigation. The only regular thing about it was the time ticking away.

He ripped open the envelope, glimpsing

Miriam Cromer's face before he turned the photograph over. Brodski's message was written unevenly in the small space under Howard Cromer's ornate imprint:

Please Mr Cribb this truth. I ask all the street. Nobody know this lady.   Brodski.

Cribb's lips tightened. He believed Brodski. The man had been badly scared. He would have supplied a name if he could. Whether his neighbours had been frank with him was less certain. Cribb had no way of finding out. He had played the trick and lost. He picked up his hat and left Scotland Yard.

He decided to walk the three miles home to Bermondsey. In his present frame of mind he would be no company for Millie.

Tomorrow was Wednesday. Unless there was a reprieve, the execution would take place on Monday morning. By now, the hangman must have received his summons. Miriam Cromer must have been moved into the condemned wing of Newgate, ready to take the short walk to the execution shed.

Unless there was a reprieve . . . A recommendation to the Queen from the Home Secretary. Something he had once heard passed through his mind, a story that Her Majesty was merciless towards miscreants of her own sex, reluctant ever to sign a reprieve. When a woman had confesed to murder, pleaded guilty and been sentenced to death, it would require more than an element of doubt to save her from the gallows. The abiding principle of British justice no longer applied in this case. Miriam

Cromer was guilty unless she was proved innocent.

In reality, Cribb had three days left. If there were grounds for a reprieve, the Home Secretary would need to know before the weekend. He would need to weigh the evidence, make consultations, reach a decision and possibly make a recommendation to the Queen.

Three days.

Darkness was closing in as he took the footway over Hungerford Bridge. The Thames, blood-red and streaked with shadows, moved soundlessly below. The boards vibrated to the rhythms of a train steaming towards Charing Cross. Billowing vapour engulfed him.

Before it cleared, he had decided how he would spend Wednesday morning.

He would begin by winning the confidence of Inspector Moser. He would make it clear that he was not asking to see the Yard's collection of confiscated prints and photographs out of prurience. Nor was he ambitious to oust Moser as the scourge of Holywell Street. He was interested only in securing evidence of blackmail.

WEDNESDAY, 20th JUNE

Inspector Moser was not easily convinced. He believed he had a responsibility to safeguard fellow officers from corruption. The pictures he confiscated were not kept in his office at the Yard. He locked them in despatch-boxes and delivered them in person to a store in the vaults of the Home Office. It was constantly manned by a store-keeper of unrelenting vigilance and failing eyesight. Moser escorted Cribb there and introduced him. This was at ten. It had taken three-quarters of an hour to win the concession.

Cribb was not shocked by the photographs the storekeeper brought out in the locked boxes. As he had patiently explained to Moser, twenty years in the force had removed any ignorance he had in the realm of sexual behaviour. Rather he found that the sheer mass of material oppressed him. Concentration was difficult as he worked steadily through everything retrieved from Holywell Street in the last twelve months. In front of him he placed the picture of Miriam Cromer. Each time he glanced at it to check whether there was the least resemblance to something from Moser's collection, he saw only her reproach.

After two and a half hours he had completed the chore. His head ached, his mouth and hands were dry with dust and he had found nothing.

He was ready to bet that the first part of that confession was a fabrication. But he had no proof. His findings were all negative. Howard Cromer had not been in Brighton on the morning of the murder. Brodski had not traced the source of the photographic plates. There was not one picture of Miriam Cromer in all Inspector Moser's haul from Holywell Street. Nothing conclusive.

From the Home Office he went directly to the public baths in Great Smith Street and took a shower. He followed it with the usual pint and pie at the Prince of Wales in Tothill Street and by 1.15 p.m. he was boarding a yellow bus in Victoria Street. It took him to Highgate.

There was nobody he knew in the police station. The sergeant on duty was busy with a complaint about damage to property, so after a word with a constable barely old enough to shave, Cribb picked up the local gazetteer and leafed through it. Among the clubs and societies he found no reference to the Highgate Literary and Artistic Society. Another negative.

He asked the constable if he had any knowledge of such an organisation. He had not. But across the room, the sergeant had caught the end of Cribb's question. 'Hold on, will you? I can tell you a bit about that lot when I've dealt with this.'

Cribb waited twenty minutes, powerless to point out that in Newgate the minutes of a woman's life were numbered. The breaking of a few windows in Southwood Lane took precedence here.

'There *was* a society of that name,' he learned at last. 'They stopped meeting two or three years ago over some disagreement among the members. A group of them formed another society, but it didn't last more than a month or two. It wouldn't, without Mrs Davenant. She ran the original society single-handed – hired the speakers, booked the rooms, collected the subscriptions, paid the bills. They didn't need a committee.'

'Is this lady still alive?'

'Good Lord, yes, and don't we know it! She runs the Watch Committee now.'

'Single-handed?'

'You would think so.'

'Where can I find Mrs Davenant?'

'What day is it? Wednesday. Try the Board School two hundred yards up the road. She likes to visit the schools once a month to see the state of the children's heads. Public hygiene is another of her interests.'

So it was that Cribb presently found himself conducting a conversation with the enterprising Mrs Davenant across a succession of small cropped heads. Her own was sensibly covered for the exercise in something like a beekeeper's bonnet, but enough of her face was visible through the muslin for Cribb to see that it was extensively lined, and every line contributed to an expression of iron determination.

'This is about the woman in Kew, is it not?' she said as soon as Cribb mentioned the Literary and Artistic Society. 'That creature who poisoned a man. It was all in *The Times*. Lies!'

'Lies, ma'am?'

'That vile confession. A concoction of wicked lies. Mentioning *my* society in such a connection! I can tell you that I saw my solicitor as soon as I read the report. I wanted to sue, naturally, but he informs me that there is no possibility of legal redress. I am prevented from defending my own reputation. You would think from *The Times* that the Society existed for no other purpose than the debauching of innocent girls. Next.'

Another head arrived for inspection.

'Do you recollect Mrs Miriam Cromer as a member of the Society, ma'am?'

'I do not.'

'It was six years ago, of course,' said Cribb. 'She was just a girl of twenty then, known by her maiden name of Kilpatrick. I have a photograph of her which may assist your memory.'

'My memory requires no assistance,' said Mrs Davenant, pushing the child away and beckoning the next. 'And photographs, in my experience, distort the countenance beyond recognition.'

'She referred in her confession to two friends,' Cribb persisted. 'Perhaps you would remember three girls of about the same age coming to the meetings?'

Mrs Davenant denied it. She denied everything but the Society's existence. If he was to make any headway at all, Cribb had to start with that.

'When was the Society formed?'

'In April, 1881, the month poor Disraeli passed on. *There* was a prime minister! A lady would not be prevented from defending herself against libellous attacks in dear Dizzie's day, I assure you. Not only was he a gentleman and a statesman second to none, but a literary man. For our inaugural meeting we had a Disraeli evening, as a mark of respect, with readings from *Coningsby* and *Sybil*. Next.'

'I expect you had a good attendance for that.'

'Thirty or forty, certainly,' said Mrs Davenant. 'The total membership was over eighty by the end of the year, although not all were regular attenders.'

'This must be a very cultured part of the capital,' Cribb commented. 'There's nothing like that in Bermondsey, where I live. You wouldn't get half a dozen to a meeting.'

'If that is intended as a personal challenge, my man, you may wish to be informed that I have drawn audiences in excess of a hundred to temperance meetings in localities as benighted as Bow and Bethnal Green. Don't underestimate Dorothea Davenant.'

'On the contrary,' said Cribb. 'I was reliably informed that the Society existed entirely through your inspiration and unflagging enterprise, ma'am.'

For a second she rested her hands on the child's head and smiled. 'One tries to occupy oneself usefully, Sergeant.'

'Highgate should be grateful.'

'Not only Highgate,' said Mrs Davenant. 'Hampstead, Finchley, Muswell Hill and Crouch End. My membership list was a testimony to the Society's reputation in North London.'

Seizing the chance he had been fencing for,

Cribb asked, 'Do you by any chance still have that list, ma'am?'

'Destroyed,' said Mrs Davenant firmly. 'When the Society came to an end, I put everything to the flame, correspondence, accounts, reports of meetings, everything. I was extremely provoked, as you may imagine. Certain people had taken it upon themselves to make a personal attack on my management. They accused me of self-aggrandisement, Sergeant! I thought that was so despicable that I resigned my position and told them to manage the Society exactly as they wished. Of course it ceased to function. Highgate was deprived of culture by the vitriolic remarks of a clique of jealous incompetents. Headmaster!' she called over the child's head. 'There appears to be something here. Have the doctor look at it, will you?'

'That's sad,' said Cribb, 'that a fine society like that should disappear overnight. Memories apart, there's nothing to prove that it ever existed?'

'Not a thing.'

Someone gave a slight cough at Cribb's elbow. It was the headmaster, small, pale and white-haired. 'Pardon me, Mrs Davenant, but I couldn't help overhearing what you said. If this gentleman is looking for proof of the Society's existence, I have it in my study. If you recall, I was a loyal attender for three years. When we made our little pilgrimage to Hampstead to look at the seat at the end of Well Walk where poor John Keats was accustomed to rest before he died, we all formed up for a photograph prior to our picnic and poetry recitation – do you remember? Well, I purchased a copy as a memento of the afternoon I discovered the romantic poets. Their verse has sustained me through my attacks of melancholia ever since. If this picture is of any interest, sir – '

'I should like to see it,' said Cribb. 'Would you excuse me, ma'am?'

'Please yourself,' said Mrs Davenant, seizing another head. 'I have more vital things to attend to than photographs.'

The picture hung in a centre position on the wall facing the headmaster's desk. It showed about thirty people in summer clothes, some standing, others seated, against a background of elm trees. The definition was moderately good, good enough, anyway, for Mrs Davenant to be recognisable in a hat the size of a parasol. Others in the party, in particular those in full sunlight, were less easy to distinguish. Closely as Cribb peered, he could not discover anyone he would swear was Miriam Cromer.

'These people on the left didn't come out so well,' he said. 'You wouldn't remember who they were, I suppose, sir?'

'I am afraid not. This was taken six years ago, in the summer of 1882,' said the head-master. 'Unhappily it has faded, being in a position that catches the sun. Candidly, I doubt whether I should know their names if the faces were clearer. The membership of the Society could not be described as stable. Mrs Davenant was indefatigable in her efforts to recruit, but many lasted as members for only a week. The programme of lectures was perhaps too narrow for certain tastes. No, most of these people are strangers to me.'

Cribb was trying not to feel persecuted. To have found the photograph and still be unable to identify the people in it was damnably frustrating. 'It just occurs to me,' he said before admitting defeat, 'that in group portraits the names are sometimes written on the reverse, to assist identification. I wonder whether –'

'There's nothing on the reverse of this,' said the headmaster. 'Look.' He lifted the frame off its hook and turned it for Cribb to examine. It was lined with plain brown paper.

Cribb took out a pocket knife. 'You don't mind, sir?' Before the headmaster could answer there was a neat incision round three sides of the paper. Cribb folded it back and removed the backing of thin wood. 'How about that, then?'

The picnickers were listed on the back of the mount in fine copperplate and Cribb's eye had picked out the name *Miss M. Kilpatrick* immediately. She was one of the group on the left blanched by sunlight. He turned the photograph and made out two female figures seated on a log and another standing near them. In front, two males in blazers and straw hats reclined on the ground. Their names, apart from Miriam's, were Miss J. Honeycutt, Miss C. Piper, Mr G. Swinson and Mr S. Allingham.

His mind reeling with the implications, Cribb asked, 'Do you remember any of these people now we have their names, sir?'

'Absolutely not,' the headmaster answered in a tone that left no doubt of his displeasure at the mutilation of his picture.

'Then perhaps you keep a copy of Kelly's? I shall not damage one page of it, you have my word.'

The school copy of the *Post Office Directory of London* was five years old but it would do for Cribb's purpose. He turned up Hampstead and began running his thumb down the street-list. He was looking for the name of Honeycutt. It was less common than Piper and should be easy to spot. If there was a Honeycutt in Hampstead, the chance was high that he would have found the address of one of Miriam's friends. He saw it on the fifth page. James Honeycutt was an umbrella maker of Flask Walk.

Cribb muttered his thanks, jammed on his bowler, went out into the High Street and gave a piercing whistle. This contingency merited a cab. As it bowled across the Heath he sat well back, ignoring the scene. He was deciding how to broach the subject of indecent photographs with Miss J. Honeycutt.

Flask Walk was on the left at the lower end of Hampstead High Street. Cribb paid the cabby and marched up the middle of the narrow street looking for the umbrella shop. He reached the end without finding it. Cursing his luck, he went into a bookshop to inquire. Honeycutt's, he learned, had closed down three years ago. The premises were now occupied by an ironmongers. He crossed the Walk to see if the present owner could tell him the whereabouts of the family.

'The Honeycutts? Couldn't say, sir. There was only the old man left, wasn't there? He wasn't up to carrying on the business after his daughter went.'

'She went, you say? Where did she go?'

'To meet her Maker. She died, sir. Suicide, it was. She took poison. A tragedy. She was only twenty-one, and a fine-looking lass, too.'

'When did this happen?'

'It must have been three or four months before the old man sold up his business. Yes, I would say it was August or September, 1884. It was all reported in the *Express* at the time.'

It was from the file of the *Hampstead and Highgate Express* in their office at Holly Mount that Cribb obtained a fuller account of Judith Honeycutt's death:

THE HAMPSTEAD POISONING TRAGEDY

Mr Adolphus, the North London Coroner, held an inquest on Monday last at the Civic Hall touching on the death of Judith May Honeycutt, aged twenty-one years, a spinster lately residing at Flask Walk, Hampstead, who was found dead on 31st August in the studio of Mr Julian Ducane, photographer, of West End Lane, West Hampstead. Mr Ducane deposed that the deceased had been in his employment as a retoucher and receptionist since March. On the Friday in question he had left her working in the studio while he went to Swiss Cottage to collect some materials. Upon his return at about a quarter to five o'clock, Mr Ducane discovered the deceased lying dead beside the desk where she had been working. From the attitude of the body, he suspected she had taken poison. A teacup was found beside the body.

Dr Pearson Stuart, principal pathologist at Haverstock Hill Infirmary, stated that he had conducted a post mortem examination and found traces of potassium cyanide. Tests he had carried out indicated that the deceased had swallowed approximately 10 grains, which must have induced rapid paralysis and death. Traces of the substance were also found in the cup, which had contained tea. In further evidence Dr Stuart stated that the deceased was three months *enceinte* at the time of death.

Miss C. Piper, of Kidderpore Avenue, friend of the deceased, stated that she had seen her the day before and found her in a cheerful frame of mind, despite her condition.

Mr Ducane, recalled, said that he had been unaware of the deceased's condition. He had always found her a reliable employee. In response to a question from the Coroner he stated that potassium cyanide was used in the developing process of photography and a bottle was kept on an open shelf in the studio. It was marked with a poison label.

In his final address the Coroner said that

the evidence indicated that the deceased had taken her own life. Although a witness had testified that the deceased had declared herself unconcerned about her condition, it was possible that this was from bravado, to conceal her anxiety. The Coroner took the opportunity to comment that Mr Ducane had demonstrated lamentable negligence in keeping a deadly poison on an open shelf. While he could not have anticipated the tragedy as it had occurred, it was a matter for regret that the agent of Miss Honeycutt's destruction had been so readily to hand.

The jury, on the coroner's advice, returned a verdict of suicide.

Towards 5 p.m. the Manchester to Euston Express steamed through South Hampstead on the London and North Western Railway. In a second-class compartment of the third carriage, James Berry folded his newspaper and stood to put it in his Gladstone bag on the luggage rack. Seconds later the train entered Primrose Hill Tunnel. It had been a journey in keeping with the slogan of the L.N.W.R. – *Noted for Punctuality, Speed, Smooth Riding, Dustless Tracks, Safety and Comfort.* Moreover, not one of his fellow-passengers had recognised him. He had not been bothered with people goggling at him from the corridor or asking idiot questions about the contents of his bag.

Nor were there newspaper reporters on the platform at Euston to pester him. Coming down to London two days earlier had definite advantages. Instead of the usual pantomime of changing cabs and doubling back to give the press the slip, he was able to take a leisurely ride by the direct route to his usual lodging in Wardrobe Place, off Carter Lane, which he always found convenient for his work, being just up the hill from Newgate, right in the shadow of St Paul's.

The press had never succeeded in tracing him to Mrs Meacham's. He had made it his rule when visiting the prison to approach it indirectly walking the wrong way up Ludgate Hill and cutting through Bread Street to Cheapside and so down to Newgate Street. He could not avoid them at the prison gate, but they had not the slightest notion where he had come from. When he came out, if he suspected he was being followed, he took a couple of turns round St Paul's and dodged out by the southwest door, under the clocktower. They didn't reckon on a hangman visiting a cathedral.

This Wednesday afternoon, though, he arrived in style in Wardrobe Place, and gave the cabman a threepenny tip for helping him with his baggage. Mrs M. had tripe and onions cooking. She greeted him by name. He had never stooped to using a false identity with her. She was a fine woman, no busybody. She had never made inquiry as to the purpose of his visits to London, though he would have been surprised if she had not guessed by now.

After the meal he took a quiet walk round the City and retired early. Thursday would be an important day.

THURSDAY, 21st JUNE

It took him first to Tussaud's. He travelled by the underground railway to Baker Street, a journey that recaptured in smells and sounds his first visit, as a lad twenty years before. Since then London had shrunk in his mind to Euston Station, Mrs Meacham's and the execution shed.

He arrived an hour before his appointment, for a good reason. He wanted to take a quiet look round before he met Mr Tussaud. So he paid his shilling at the turnstile like everyone else.

He was pleased to note that the Exhibition had moved from the old Baker Street Rooms into more commodious premises in the Marylebone Road. It was altogether more palatial than he remembered. He mounted a marble staircase into the Hall of Kings, a dazzling place with Richard the Lionheart, Henry and his six wives and every crowned head up to her Imperial Majesty. He felt a tremor of pride at joining them, albeit in a different room. The figures were so finely modelled that he might have walked up and introduced himself. Most riveting of all was a tableau of the Prince of Wales tiger-hunting on his Indian tour. His Royal Highness was up there on a howdah on the back of a stuffed elephant. He was in the attitude of firing both barrels into a tiger which his mount had cleverly pinned to the ground. Berry stood in front of the exhibit and imagined himself aiming the shotgun.

His steps took him next past the statesmen

of the civilised world to the Chamber of Horrors, for which he discovered he had to pay sixpence more. That amused him. You could see the Royals and Mr Gladstone, Lord Beaconsfield and President Lincoln for a shilling, but to clap eyes on Burke and Hare and their companions it was a tanner extra. No-one seemed to mind stumping up. Only a few faint hearts waited upstairs while their bolder escorts had sixpennyworth of horrors.

The Chamber was cunningly lit with mantles of coloured glass set low on the wall to give a more horrid aspect to the figures. It was smaller down there than Berry expected. Quite a crush, in fact. The attendant kept asking people to move along as they came to the notorieties in the dock: Palmer, Peace, Kate Webster, Muller, Lefroy and the rest. The lighting apart, nothing had been done to make the figures grotesque. Most of them looked unexceptional. Murderers generally were, in Berry's experience. There were faces more villainous among the public filing past. The horror lay in discovering that those they had come to see were no different from anyone else.

He soon found Bill Marwood – his effigy, that is to say. It was a marvellous likeness. The eyes had that mild, almost dreamy look and the mouth was set in a downward curve that followed the line of the tobacco-stained moustache. He was in his own black bow and stand-up collar. Marwood to the life. The only fault was that he was holding the pinioning-strap all wrong, more like a butler with a tray than a hangman ready for work. This technicality did not disappoint those who had come to look. Out of interest, Berry lingered close to the figure to eavesdrop on the comments. Curiously, Bill Marwood with his strap had a more chilling effect than all the murderers together. One young woman visibly shuddered at the sight of him. 'Don't be alarmed, dearest,' her chinless escort said. 'That is only Marwood. He is dead. Berry has the job now.'

He decided against introducing himself.

So, fresh from seeing the show, he went back to the entrance at half past ten to keep his appointment. Mr Joseph Tussaud, grandson of the Exhibition's founder, his son, John, and five others were waiting in an office. Berry guessed that most of them were there to say that they had shaken him by the hand, which they did, to a man. There was not much said. One of them asked him if it had been raining in Yorkshire. Champagne was served by a liveried footman. Then Mr Tussaud Senior proposed a tour of the Exhibition. It would have been discourteous to disclose that he had just been round it.

Actually he was glad of the conducted tour, because he learned a lot from Mr Tussaud. The Chamber of Horrors was closed to the public for half an hour to allow the official party a private view. It was like being the Prince of Wales.

He found the place noticeably more gruesome this time. The glass eyes of the figures seemed to watch his approach and move with him. Mr Tussaud told him that visitors were sometimes convinced one of the figures had moved, and they were right, because the Metropolitan Line was sited below the Chamber and sometimes caused vibrations.

They told him he would always be welcome there. Bill Marwood and the grizzled old mongrel he had kept as a pet had been frequent visitors. They knew Marwood's taste for gin and had always provided him with a glass and a pipe of tobacco.

Berry wanted to be satisfied that they would exhibit his model like Marwood's, in a position that made it clear that he was not a lawbreaker, so he raised the matter with Mr Tussaud. 'I should not wish to be an object of abomination and disgust,' he said pointedly.

Mr Tussaud drew back in surprise. 'My dear Berry, you need have no anxiety on that score,' he answered. 'Mr Marwood selected the spot where he wished his figure to stand and so shall you. But even if by some mischance your likeness was taken for a murderer, I doubt very much whether it would excite the emotions you describe. Far from disgust, our patrons tend to regard the figures with awe and veneration. This may surprise you, but when we remove the clothes from the models to clean them, we often find handkerchiefs in the pockets. They are ladies' handkerchiefs, lace-edged and still smelling of perfume.'

It did not surprise him. He had long since ceased being surprised by the morbid inclinations of the fair sex. He had not forgotten that his business in London this time was with one of them. Nor had Mr Tussaud.

When the tour was done, the guests shook his hand again and departed. He was taken to the modelling-room. He saw scores of disembodied heads ranged on shelves along the walls. Some he recognised from newspaper illustrations. He supposed Marwood's head would soon be deposited there. 'This place is grimmer than the Chamber of Horrors,' he told his host.

They told him how the figures were modelled, using clay, from which a plaster cast was made. The wax was poured into the mould so formed. When it had hardened, the plaster was removed. The wax did not come into contact with the sitter. All that was required were measurements and sketches and a degree of patience while the head was modelled.

A fee was discussed. It was higher than he had expected. He betrayed no sign that he was pleased. They added another guinea and he accepted. 'This is a departure from custom, you will appreciate,' said Mr Tussaud. 'Those who appear in the Chamber are not usually compensated for the honour.' There was a gleam of humour in his eye.

The conversation turned quite naturally to the Kew poisoning case. 'Our model of Miriam Cromer is practically finished,' said Mr Tussaud. 'Now that public executions are discontinued, the crowds come here on the morning of a hanging instead of gathering in front of Newgate. We exhibit the figure of the murderer immediately we hear that you have performed your work. A notorious murderer will attract twenty thousand or more. The street outside is impassable for hours. A murderess is a particular attraction. Miriam Cromer had no trial to speak of but I still expect a considerable crowd on Monday morning.'

'It's just a job to me,' Berry made clear. 'I make no distinction, man or woman, except in calculating the drop.'

'I understand that a petition with over ten thousand signatures is to be delivered to the Home Office,' said Mr Tussaud. 'There is a lot of sympathy for Mrs Cromer. The columns of the newspapers are daily filled with correspondence about the sentence.'

'That's to be expected,' Berry told him. 'By all accounts, she's a good-looking woman, and she was being blackmailed. The public are easily swayed by sentiment.'

'Shall you see her before Monday morning?'

'It's my custom to visit them in the condemned cell the day previous. They like to be assured that I do my work without causing them to suffer. It's thirteen years since Calcraft retired, but the stories of his bunglings persist.'

'Mr Marwood used to tell us,' said Mr Tussaud quickly.

'Every word were true,' Berry went on. 'When I were in Bradford and West Riding Police I saw the old man turn off three together in Manchester. He were over seventy then. Forty years and more as public hangman. He had to climb on the back of one to finish him. Strangulation. It should never happen. Marwood changed all that. It's scientific now. We give them a long drop.' He talked about his

144

table of body weights, but Mr Tussaud found he had something urgent to attend to elsewhere in the building, so Berry was left in the care of the young man working the clay.

It was a long sitting, but by the end a tolerable likeness emerged. You could not really judge, the young sculptor said, until the eyeballs were in and the hair and moustaches on. Perhaps not, but what was there already was right. Looked at from the side, the face had what his mother used to call the Berry profile, the strong forehead, straight nose and firm jawline. He liked it enough for the thought to enter his mind of asking them to model two and give him the spare to bring home. Just the head.

Thinking it over, he decided against the idea. True, his wife had said she would like his portrait in the front room, but he suspected she would not feel easy with his head in wax, even under a glass dome. Besides, there could be a difficulty travelling with it. He could carry it wrapped in a hatbox, but there were always people ready to put grisly misconstructions on things. If he planned a surprise like that, something was sure to go wrong. He dared not take the risk.

No, the surprise he originally had planned was better. He would have his photograph done in London and take it home as a present. His wife would take it as such, any road. For himself, if things went according to plan, it would be a souvenir fit to take its place in the front room with the great knife used by the executioner of Canton and his other relics.

He was going out to Kew to have his portrait taken by Mr Howard Cromer.

Before lunch, Mr Tussaud returned and some further business was discussed. An offer was made for certain items shortly to come into Berry's possession. He promised to give the matter his consideration. He would sleep on it and give them an answer in the morning, when he came for another sitting.

Mr Tussaud said that they would put Berry's figure in the Exhibition on Monday morning. If he had occasion to drop by, he could see it before returning to Bradford. Berry smiled and made no promises.

'There were these three young ladies,' said Chief Inspector Jowett.

It might have been the start of a smoking-room story, except that this was Sergeant Cribb's sitting room in George Road, Bermondsey, and Jowett never told stories to lower ranks. He was putting some order into the verbal report he had just received from Cribb. That was how he would have expressed it, if pressed. Cribb had his own idea what was going on. Jowett had caught the scent of a decision ahead. If he could find a way of avoiding it, he would.

'Miriam Kilpatrick, Judith Honeycutt and Miss C. Piper,' said Cribb.

'And you believe that because they were photographed together on the Literary and Artistic Society outing, they were the three who were tricked into posing for offensive photographs?'

'The confession mentioned three,' said Cribb, sidestepping the question.

'So you went in search of Judith Honeycutt and found that she was dead?'

'From cyanide poisoning.'

'The significance had not escaped me, Cribb,' said Jowett stiffly. 'But she *was* employed as a photographer's assistant. We know that potassium cyanide is used in photography. It is not uncommonly used by people committing suicide. We must beware of reading too much into this. Coincidence is a snare, Sergeant, a snare.'

'If it was just one coincidence . . .' said Cribb.

Jowett reddened. 'Are you keeping something from me, Sergeant?'

'I was coming to it, sir.'

'Well?'

'I was interested in the photographer who employed Miss Honeycutt.'

'Ducane? How is he significant?'

'I thought he might be able to tell me some more about the circumstances of Miss Honeycutt's death.'

Jowett took out his pipe and knocked it noisily on Cribb's mantelpiece. 'Dammit, Cribb, isn't it enough to know that the girl is dead? Our job is to inquire into Perceval's death and there's precious little time left for that.'

'I'm aware of that, sir,' Cribb said thickly. 'I'm endeavouring to keep my report as short as possible.'

Jowett sighed and stuffed tobacco into the pipe. 'Get on with it, then.'

'I decided to go to West Hampstead, with

the intention of calling on Mr Ducane. I found the road all right, but I couldn't find the studio.'

'He had sold the business and left, I suppose,' said Jowett in a voice that had already moved on to other things.

'Yes, sir. I talked to several of his former neighbours. There was plenty of sympathy for him in West End Lane, but he still lost most of his clients. You know how people are about photography. It's enough of an ordeal having your portrait done, without going to a place visited by tragedy. Ducane waited only a few weeks, realised he was finished in Hampstead and sold the premises to an optician. Nobody could tell me what happened to him after that, but I had a theory of my own. I asked what Ducane had looked like, and between them they supplied me with a serviceable description. Five foot seven or eight. Medium build. Dark hair going grey. Brown eyes. Dapper in his dress. Aged thirty-eight or so.'

'I don't call that serviceable,' said Jowett scornfully. 'I could go out now and find you a dozen men like that inside ten minutes.'

'Not in Bermondsey,' said Cribb. 'You don't get nobby dressers in this locality, sir. I'll grant you there are no other outstanding characteristics in the description, but at least it didn't conflict with my theory.'

'Which is . . . ?'

'That after Julian Ducane left Hampstead, he started up again as a photographer in Kew.'

'My word! Howard Cromer?'

'Look at it from Ducane's point of view,' said

Cribb. 'His business was in danger of collapse if he stayed in Hampstead, so he got out as quickly as he decently could. With his savings and the money from the sale of his studio he could afford to start again in another well-heeled locality. Obviously he didn't want people to know what had happened in Hampstead, so he chose to live on the other side of London, across the river. And to make sure, I believe he changed his name.'

Jowett simply stared at Cribb, holding his unlighted pipe an inch from his mouth.

'When I interviewed Howard Cromer earlier this week,' Cribb continued, 'he went to no end of trouble to co-operate – showed me over the studio, talked about his wife and got out their family photograph album. I'm not used to being treated like that by people of his sort, who like to think they have arrived in society. Usually as soon as I give my rank, it's "Very well, officer, go to the kitchen and ask cook to give you a mug of tea and I'll answer your questions when I can spare a minute." I couldn't decide what Cromer was up to – trying to sweeten me or lead me up the garden path. I'm inclined to think it was both. He didn't lie to me exactly, but some of his statements could only be described as misleading, and that's charitable. I wanted to find out which train he caught to Brighton on the day of the murder. I couldn't get a straight answer, except that he left the house before ten. He may have done, but the fact is that he wasn't expected in Brighton till half past two.'

'There may be an innocent explanation for that,' Jowett pointed out. 'What was the phrase he used in the letter to the Portrait Photographers' League?'

'*Prevented by another commitment.*'

'Have you asked him what the commitment was?'

'I haven't talked to him since Sunday, sir.' Cribb pretended not to notice one of the Chief Inspector's eyebrows shoot up. If Jowett wanted to criticise his conduct of the case, he could damned well come out with it in plain English. 'But that wasn't the only statement intended to mislead me. When he showed me the photograph album, he tried to give me the impression he first met Miriam in April, 1885, on the day her father brought the family to the studio at Kew for a group portrait. I believe he must have known her three years earlier than that.'

'Really?' Jowett sounded unconvinced. 'What grounds do you have for saying that?'

'First, I was suspicious of the album itself, sir. I noticed two of the pages were stuck together. Cromer had to separate them with a knife. He said something about glue on the mount, but as it was a photograph of the wedding, two and a half years ago, I couldn't understand how glue had got on to it unless it had recently been pasted into the album. That set me thinking that he might have put the entire album together in the last day or so in order to illustrate his story, the story he wanted me to believe. He put the damned thing into my hands at the first opportunity, telling me it was his most precious possession. Naturally the first picture in it was the portrait of the Kilpatrick family.'

'That's a lot to deduce from one spot of glue, Sergeant.'

'It isn't the only thing, sir. There's the matter of the photograph the headmaster showed me. The picnic outing on Hampstead Heath. It showed the three girls together, and beside them was Simon Allingham, Cromer's oldest friend. If Allingham was known to Miriam in the summer of 1882 – '

'That's speculation,' cut in Jowett and there was a disagreeable note of triumph in his voice. 'We cannot draw any such conclusion. The mere fact that they were situated in some proximity in a photograph could be accidental. There is no guarantee that the Allingham in the picture is the same person, since you admitted yourself that the figures were unrecognisable. It won't do, Sergeant. Do you know what you are guilty of?' Jowett jabbed his pipe-stem at Cribb. '*Post hoc ergo propter hoc.* Do you have Latin? No matter. In short, your reasoning is founded on a fallacy. You have persuaded yourself that Cromer is not what he purports to be and you are fitting the facts to justify your prejudice.'

'It's true there isn't concrete evidence – ' Cribb began.

'Evidence of what?' crowed Jowett without pausing for an answer. 'That Howard Cromer was formerly known as Julian Ducane? Is that what you hope to prove, Sergeant? Even if he was, there is nothing very sinister in it, is there? People in trade frequently change the names by which they are known as they move up in the world.'

'There *is* the matter of Judith Honeycutt's death.'

'Exactly! A very good reason for taking on a new name,' said Jowett. 'Frankly, if Howard Cromer was unfortunate enough to have had such a tragedy in his former establishment, it isn't surprising that he is evasive about his past.'

'He needn't have been evasive about Brighton.'

Jowett asked, 'Are you seriously telling me that you suspect him of being involved in Perceval's death?'

'It's possible, sir. If he was in Kew that morning he could have put poison into the decanter as easily as his wife could. More important, he had a key to the poison cabinet, and she didn't.'

For an interval, only the ticking of the clock was audible in the room.

'If that were true,' said Jowett, 'someone must have seen him in Park Lodge. Have you questioned the servants?'

'No help there, sir. After nine o'clock, they aren't allowed upstairs. He doesn't want clients meeting the domestics.'

Jowett eased a finger round his collar. 'It's still in the realm of speculation, then? Just a convenient theory of yours. Sergeant, I cannot emphasise too forcibly that if there is anything in this at all, it won't convince the Home Secretary without solid evidence to support it. Where is that evidence to come from?'

'Mrs Miriam Cromer.'

The chief inspector's eyes narrowed to slits. 'What precisely are you saying, Sergeant?'

'I'm saying this is Thursday, sir. The woman is due to hang on Monday. Our report should be on the Commissioner's table by tomorrow evening. You are absolutely right – I have no direct evidence that Howard Cromer was implicated in the murder. If this was a regular investigation I'd put a couple of men on house-to-house inquiries to establish Cromer's movements on the morning of the crime. *Someone* must have seen him leaving the house or walking to the station or stepping on the train. But even if I established that he was still in the house at noon, after the wine was delivered, it isn't proof that he was involved in the poisoning. It strengthens the suspicion, no more. There isn't time to carry out the exercise and, anyway, I don't have the men. I'm obliged to seek the information another way. Miriam Cromer can tell me. I want permission to interview her, sir.'

Jowett closed his eyes as people do in the split-second before an impact. A decision was unavoidable. 'To interview the prisoner herself?' he said in a whisper.

'In the time we have left, it's the only way to get at the truth, sir,' Cribb said, talking fast. 'She of all people knows what really happened. If anyone can supply the *prima facie* evidence that her husband was involved, it's her. I believe I have enough information now to justify asking her to clarify certain things in her confession. I'm not without experience in questioning witnesses. If she is lying, I'm confident I can bring it out in an interview.'

Jowett was shaking his head. 'It's out of the question.'

Controlling his voice, Cribb said, 'With respect, I should like to know why, sir.'

There was another uneasy silence.

Jowett got up from the armchair, walked to the window and looked out. 'On the slender suspicions we have, it simply isn't possible to make a formal request to the governor of Newgate for an interview with Mrs Cromer. It would not be countenanced. There is no chance of it.'

'Surely in the interests of justice – '

'Justice has had its opportunity, Sergeant. There are other interests to be considered now, not least the state of mind of the prisoner. Miriam Cromer expects to die. Prisoners under sentence of death are not encouraged to entertain the slightest hope of a reprieve. It is easier for everyone concerned if they philosophically accept the inevitable. You must understand yourself that an intervention from us could have a most unsettling effect on the woman.'

The inevitable.

Cribb stared at Jowett's back, feeling the force of what had been said. The glib phrases echoed in his head.

Justice has had its opportunity . . . other in-

terests to be considered . . . easier for everyone concerned.

There was more, much more, behind this than Jowett's inertia.

'I don't know if I understand you, sir. Are you telling me that there is no combination of circumstances that would make it possible for me to question Mrs Cromer?'

Without turning, Jowett answered, 'Sergeant, I don't altogether care for that question. It is not for you to speculate on a matter that I made quite clear is not within police jurisdiction.'

'I asked because I need to know how to proceed,' said Cribb flatly.

Jowett's frame stiffened. Cribb had defused the rebuke with a valid point. 'It would be wise, I think, to address yourself to the matter of the key to the poison cabinet. That, after all, occasioned this inquiry. These other matters you have mentioned have not altered the significance of that.'

Cribb's eyes widened. Had he not made it crystal clear that he suspected Howard Cromer of opening the cabinet with his own key?

Jowett turned from the window, spreading his hands expansively, yet there was a look in his eyes that he tried not to have there.

'In short, Cribb, we are required to find out how she did it. Do you follow?'

Cribb followed. This was no inquiry at all. It was an exercise in politics. The Home Office wanted an explanation of the photograph of Cromer wearing his key at Brighton. An explanation that did not conflict with the confession. The Commissioner had handed the job to Jowett, the chief inspector with an unequalled reputation for paperwork. Jowett would oblige and they would hang Miriam Cromer. After the execution, if anyone raised the question of her guilt, the Home Secretary could stand up in the House and say that he had ordered an independent inquiry after the trial and it had not conflicted with the facts as set out in the confession.

Cribb moistened his lips, scarcely trusting himself to speak. 'I think I understand your meaning, sir.'

'I'm glad we are of one mind,' said Jowett. 'I am not unappreciative of your work these last few days. If it had produced a shred of firm evidence . . .' He shrugged. 'There was so little time.'

Cribb picked up Jowett's hat. He wanted him out of his house.

'Give this business of the key some thought, then,' Jowett said, moving to the door. 'But not too long about it, eh? Come what may, I must have a report from you tomorrow.'

Cribb nodded once.

As if remembering something, Jowett turned when he was halfway downstairs. 'She *did* plead guilty. We'd get no thanks from her if we questioned the verdict. Best let Berry do his work on Monday and we can all heave a sigh of relief.'

'I have good news for you,' said Bell.

The prisoner looked up from her book, a glimmer of interest in her eyes. She made no response.

Bell looked across at Hawkins and rolled her eyes upwards in her long-suffering look. She planted her sewing-basket on the table and re-positioned the stool the wardress on the last turn had just vacated. She was in no hurry to surrender the information.

The prisoner waited expressionlessly.

'You want to hear what it is?'

Bell received the gratification of a nod.

'There's a visitor downstairs.' She took her calico traycloth from the basket and shook it with such vigour that it made a sound like a whip. 'I should finish this by Monday,' she told Hawkins. From the corner of her eye she watched the prisoner's lips part as if to ask the obvious. Yet the instant Bell turned in antici-pation, the mouth closed again, defying her. Their eyes met. 'You have some hair showing,' Bell said, refusing to be bested. 'Tuck it under your cap.'

Cromer obeyed. She did everything they asked, scrubbed the cell, folded her bedding, washed the tin plate, emptied the slops. They could not criticise her conduct. It was the ex-pression on her face that provoked, and even that was difficult to account for. It was not a brassy look, like some prisoners gave, not holier-than-thou even. No, what was insulting about it was that she treated the officers as if they were not there. She excluded them from her thoughts.

'Your husband,' Bell said.

She lowered her eyes to the book.

Bell clicked her tongue and started sorting through the sewing-basket for a thimble. Privately she expected this wall of indifference would topple before the weekend. There were indications already. The wardresses on nights had noticed the prisoner saying things in her sleep, whimpering sometimes and calling out. Inside herself, she was more jumpy than she wanted anyone to know.

Bell was curious to see the husband. He visited Newgate daily, but always late in the afternoon, when Officers Davis and Manks were on duty. There was a story that the first time he had brought a dozen red roses and a nightdress from Swan and Edgar which had been impounded at the prison entrance. It was a mystery to Bell how women without an ounce of passion seemed to draw the devotion of decent men. Her own experiences with the sex were bitter without exception.

Miss Stones unlocked the cell door and brought him in, a worried, pale-complexioned man in a dark suit with his hands clasped tightly in front of him. A large spotted cravat and matching handkerchief tucked into his breast-pocket must have served as emblems of artistry in Kew Green. In Newgate they were so misplaced as to seem clownish. Poor devil – he looked twenty years older than she. Silver-haired, almost, and hollow-eyed. It was the relatives who suffered most, and no mistake.

Cromer had not even stood up to greet him.

To Bell it appeared that all Howard Cromer got in the way of a greeting from his wife was a head-to-foot inspection with the ice-blue eyes. He stood just inside the door, unfastening his hands and fingering his shirt-cuffs.

Hawkins brought the spare stool to the table.

'My love – ' the man began.

'Save your love, Howard, and tell me what is happening outside,' the prisoner said as if she was talking to a servant.

'Yes, of course.' His mouth twitched into something like a smile. 'The petition is being delivered to the Home Office this afternoon. We have thirteen thousand signatures demanding a reprieve. The committee have been tireless in their efforts. There is a public meeting tomorrow on Richmond Green and we are promised a speaker from the Howard Association. I am certain thousands will come. There is a veritable avalanche of sympathy. This morning the postman simply upended a sack of letters – '

'Sympathy?' she said in a disbelieving voice. 'What do you mean – sympathy? I am not dead.'

His hand went to his neck and clutched it. 'Forgive me, Miriam, dearest. This is a testing time for us all. If you can be patient, my angel, I am confident that justice will be done. I mean, of course . . .' His voice trailed awkwardly away.

'I know what you meant,' the prisoner said. Silence.

The man fidgeted with his cuffs again. The prisoner scrutinised him thoughtfully.

'Howard, has something else happened?'

He nodded once and moved on the stool so that it made a piercing sound as it scraped the floor.

There was an unmistakable note of urgency as she said, 'Tell me, then, for pity's sake!'

He hesitated.

'I want to know, Howard.' This was more of an appeal than an order.

'My dear, we did not wish to raise your expectations prematurely, so I said nothing of this before. It is so easy, you see, to place a significance on things when we are hoping for developments as we are. It could be self-deceiving. Before speaking to you, I wanted to be sure in my own mind that this *is* significant. Today I am convinced of it, and so is Simon.' He leaned towards her, resting his hands on the table between them. 'This week I have received two visitors. On Sunday a detective sergeant came, as he put it, to dot "i"'s and cross "t"'s — in other words, to check your statement. He put some very searching questions to me and asked me to show him everything, the processing room, the studio. Believe me, he missed nothing. I showed him our album, the mother-of-pearl one, and he took away a photograph of you.'

She frowned slightly. 'Why should he want a photograph?'

'He didn't say exactly. It was a *carte* of my

favourite, the portrait of you in the black gown looking so magnificent.'

'I was not feeling magnificent.'

He lowered his eyelids and shook his head. 'Dearest, the image is what matters. The image. Whatever your innermost thoughts were, you looked superb.'

She displayed neither pleasure nor embarrassment at the compliment. 'What exactly did this detective ask you about?'

'Oh, everything. He was deeply interested in you. As you know, there is no topic I would rather talk about. I opened the album and there on the first page was the Kilpatrick family. I told him about your father bringing them to Kew for the portrait, and about our courtship. The pictures were all there for him to see. The fair at Hampstead. Our wedding. Trouville.'

Her mouth tightened and she said, 'Images.'

'Dearest, what do you mean?' The husband's face had creased with concern.

She shook her head. 'No matter, Howard. Tell me, when the detective had finished looking at the album, what questions did he ask?'

It was cool in the cell, but he took out a handkerchief and patted his forehead. 'Oh, questions about me – how long I had kept the studio in Kew, when I had first engaged Perceval as my assistant, and so forth. Of course he asked me about the day Perceval died. I told him I was in Brighton at the conference.'

'You told him – or did he ask?'

'I believe he asked. He wanted to know which train I caught.'

Her eyes widened. 'What answer did you give, Howard?'

He returned a quick smile. 'You know me, dearest, incorrigibly vague about such things. Then I took him to look at the studio. I showed him where the decanters were kept and told him how you filled them each Monday morning after the delivery from Morgan's. We looked at the processing room, naturally, and he asked to see inside the poison cabinet. Insisted on opening it himself with my key. I treated the fellow throughout with the utmost civility.'

'He was not hostile towards you?'

'No, I would not say so. Sharp, yes, but that was his manner, I suspect.'

'He went away satisfied?'

The husband shrugged. 'He *should* have been.'

'But you formed an impression to the contrary?' The prisoner watched him keenly. Bell had never seen her so attentive.

The husband drew himself up a little on the stool. 'Well, my dear, there has been a development since which compels me to conclude that the inquiries are continuing.'

'The second visitor you mentioned?'

'Yes. He arrived yesterday afternoon.' He beamed reassuringly. 'I wish you had seen him, Miriam. He would have amused you. Picture him in the reception room, if you can. A strongly-built fellow with a black beard and a broad face scarred down one side, and rather bulbous eyes. He was in a black suit very shiny from wear and a brand-new butterfly collar on a shirt that was frayed at the cuffs. But, my dear, this is the joke – he was wearing a policeman's boots!'

The prisoner still declined to smile. 'What did he want?'

Her husband nodded. 'That was what I asked him. Do you know what? He answered in a broad north-country accent – his smoking-party turn, I'm ready to wager – that he wished to arrange to have his "photo took". What do you think of that? For some occult reason Scotland Yard had sent this buffoon to insinuate himself into Park Lodge on the pretext of sitting for his portrait! Well, you know that I suspended work in the studio after what happened in March, except for one or two long-standing appointments. I explained this to my visitor, really to see what he would say. He told me his name was Holly and he was down from Yorkshire for a few days on business. He wanted his "photo took" as a present for his wife, and he would be obliged if I would make an exception and give him a sitting as he had come out to Kew for the purpose, on the recommendation of the proprietor of his hotel. Hotel! In those boots, he wouldn't get past the commissionaire. However, I am not one to obstruct an officer in the course of his duty, even if he does stoop to subterfuge. I entered into the spirit of the thing and invited him into the studio. As you may suppose, he wasted no time in getting the conversation round to Perceval. He professed great interest in seeing the very room where the "occurrence", as he described it, took place. I showed him everything I had shown the first detective. I could see it was all he could do to restrain himself from taking out his notebook.'

Bell glanced towards Hawkins. She had put her hand in front of her mouth. The prisoner's husband was keeping two of his listeners entertained, even if Cromer herself showed not a flicker of amusement.

'Did this man ask questions, Howard?'

'Not so many as the sergeant did on Sunday, but then he could not be so direct, or I might have guessed he was a policeman! Mainly he was interested in details of circumstances, where Perceval's body was found, where the cyanide was kept and so forth.'

'Nothing more definite?' She regarded him challengingly, as if he were responsible for the visitor's conduct.

He lifted his hands in an assuaging gesture. 'I told him everything he wanted to know, dearest. I photographed him, too, against that back-cloth of the Strand, just to humour the fellow.' He took a picture from his pocket and held it for her to see.

Bell's interest in the husband's story was so consuming that she had leaned forward to look before it dawned on her that what was happening was an infringement of regulations. 'That's not permitted, sir,' she told him. But she had caught enough of the portrait to satisfy her curiosity, a head and shoulders view of a burly, bearded fellow with eyes like pearl buttons. A memory stirred in her brain, too elusive to recapture, and not pleasant anyway. Photographs played odd tricks at times.

The prisoner commented, 'From the look of him, I would say he is more brutish than acute.'

'He had the intelligence to keep up the pretence,' her husband said. 'He gave me an address in Bradford to post the portrait to, and he insisted on paying me in advance. I expect it's the Bradford Police Station.' He tried to sound amused. 'I hope they are satisfied with the result.'

She stared at him in silence.

Lines of concern transformed his expression. 'Miriam, my darling, forgive me. I find this such an ordeal. I try to cloak my feelings in facetiousness and I know it is in appalling bad taste in the circumstances. The situation is so unnatural – seated here with a table between us. To be allowed only to look at you, not permitted even to touch your sweet hand. It is too cruel.'

She said in a voice devoid of emotion. 'You have always maintained that to look at me is all that you desire.'

He looked abashed, as if she had rebuked him. 'True, my dear. I meant it, of course, as a tribute.'

For an instant the prisoner appeared on the point of saying something, but she changed her mind, simply drew a long breath.

The husband was obviously at a loss. He filled the gap with words. 'Take heart, Miriam. These developments *must* be significant.'

'Have you spoken to Simon?' she asked.

'I have kept him fully informed, of course.'

'And what is his advice?'

'Quite simply, to wait.'

She thought a moment, frowning. 'Howard, that may not be the right thing now. What you have told me is disturbing. I cannot understand why they sent the second detective if he had no questions of any importance. The way it was done, sending a man to masquerade as a client, is suggestive of incompetence. We cannot tamely wait for someone to see sense. It may not happen in time. You must talk to Simon'.

He nodded. 'I shall go straight from here. I'll tell him what you say, depend upon it, dearest.'

'I am compelled to.'

He started to get up. 'You are never out of my thoughts, Miriam. When this is over . . .' He smiled encouragement. 'Is there anything else, my darling?'

'Yes. Ask Simon to visit me tomorrow morning. I want to speak to him. And Howard, I shall not expect to see you.'

He blinked in surprise. 'But – '

'I shall not expect to see you,' she repeated, spacing the words. 'Do you understand?'

He dipped his head quickly.

'Howard . . .'

'My dear?'

'I am grateful.'

Hawkins unlocked the door to let him out.

When it had closed again, the prisoner let her breath out slowly as if a crisis was past. She turned her book over and started to read.

Sleep had not subdued Cribb's anger. This morning in the front room the linnet was chirping and sunlight glistened on the brasses, but Jowett's words hung in the air. *'It is not for you to speculate on a matter that I made quite clear is not within police jurisdiction.'* Cribb stood motionless at the window, his mouth set in a tight line, eyes seeing nothing. The anger had turned inwards.

For a week he had been occupied in a sterile exercise. Used by politicians. Yet from the start he had realised that any outcome challenging the verdict of the court would embarrass Whitehall. They had wanted him to paper over a small crack, not bring the whole edifice crashing down. Trained as he was to work on investigative principles, he had preferred to keep an open mind about the murder. Establish the facts, root out the truth and let the politicians deal with the consequences. Greenhorn!

The wound went deeper. He had believed this case might transform his career. It hurt him to admit that now. He had supposed that seventeen years as sergeant had left him with few illusions about the future. If Millie still fondly believed someone at the Yard would soon recognise his ability, he was not so deluded. Ten years had passed since that day they had created the Criminal Investigation Department. Inspectors had been appointed to fourteen of the sixteen divisions. Of the two to which sergeants were nominated, his own was one. Why? No one had given him a straight answer. *'Keep your defaulter sheet clean, Cribb, and who knows?'* He had kept it clean for ten years, managed one of the toughest divisions in the Met, and he was still a detective sergeant. *Who knows?* If he didn't know by now, he was no detective at all.

Millie would go on hoping for a miracle: he faced facts. To the high-ups he was a natural sergeant. *'One of your door-to-door detectives, fly to everything. Not a man to waste behind a desk.'*

He had put promotion out of his mind. Yet what had happened a week ago? It had only wanted Jowett to let slip the name of Sir Charles Warren to set his pulse racing. A secret inquiry on the personal orders of the Commissioner!

The prospect of working for Warren had given him nightmares, but he had jumped at it like any pink and scrubbed probationer given his first incident to investigate. Impress Sir Charles with a few inspired deductions and promotion was in the bag. For that he was ready to face the perils of working for the Commissioner without the sanction of the Director of the C.I.D. The *real* politics – the politics of Whitehall – he had not paused to consider. He deserved to stay a sergeant.

He sighed, shook his head and turned from the window. There was nothing to be gained from self-pity. He crossed the room and opened the sideboard drawer. Pen and ink. He would write the report for Jowett and put this whole thing out of his mind. Three sheets of Millie's notepaper.

Report of an Inquiry into the Confession of Mrs Miriam Cromer to the Murder of Josiah Perceval at Park Lodge, Kew, on the 12th March, 1888.

When this was done he would take it to the Yard and afterwards cross Trafalgar Square to the Haymarket to try and get tickets for that comic opera Millie had been talking about.

How should he begin? It hardly mattered. Whatever he wrote, Jowett would revise it before it reached the Commissioner's desk.

Keep strictly to the facts.

'*1. The death by poisoning of Josiah Perceval took place at Park Lodge, Kew, on the 12th March, 1888. At the Old Bailey on the 8th June, 1888, Mrs Miriam Cromer pleaded guilty to murder and was sentenced to death.*

'*2. Subsequent to the trial a photo-engraving cut from a photographic journal was received at the Home Office. It showed the husband of the prisoner at Brighton on the day of the murder wearing a key on his watch-chain which was established as being one of two keys to the poison cabinet. The other was found on the body of the deceased. The question arose as to how the prisoner had unlocked the poison cabinet on the day of the crime, as she had stated in her confession. An inquiry was ordered into the events described by the prisoner in her confession, Chief Inspector Jowett of the Criminal Investigation Department leading, assisted by*

A. Cribb, Detective Sergeant, First Class, M Division.'

Cribb paused, absently touching his lips with the end of the pen. The easy bit was done. The correct procedure now was to take the confession point by point. He got up from the table and went to the shelf where he kept his papers, weighted by the black-bound *Metropolitan Police Acts*. Something fluttered to the floor. Millie *would* put her scrapbook cuttings among his things. He picked it up, a picture of some actor clipped from the *Penny Illustrated Paper*, and slipped it under the cover of her book. He found his copy of the confession and put it on the table. Would he require anything else? *Nuttall's Standard Dictionary*, for certain.

At the table again, his eyes ran through the first paragraph of Miriam Cromer's confession. A general statement of her guilt. No comment necessary on that. Second paragraph.

'Some time in 1882, when I was twenty years of age and lived at my family home in Hampstead, I injudiciously agreed to take part with two friends in a group photograph . . .'

Two friends. Judith Honeycutt, now dead, and Miss C. Piper.

The newspaper report of the inquest on Judith Honeycutt had given Miss Piper's address at Kidderpore Avenue. It was a long street in West Hampstead, off the Finchley Road. Cribb had gone there on Wednesday evening after making his inquiries about Ducane. No family by the name of Piper was known in Kidderpore Avenue. Somebody had suggested

Miss Piper might have been the young lady who had lodged at old Miss Marchant's for a few months. She had been about twenty and had come there after a disagreement of some sort with her family. She had not stayed long. By 1885 she had moved out of London. And Miss Marchant had died soon after. The house was now occupied by a family of Russian immigrants. They had no forwarding address for Miss Piper. Cribb had abandoned the search. There were scores of people with that name in London, hundreds throughout the provinces. He remembered a C.S.M. Piper from his army days, and a pet shop in Islington called Piper and Son. Hopeless, trying to locate one girl with that name in the short time left to him. He did not even know her Christian name. She could be married by now.

Wherever she was, soon after eight on Monday morning she would be the sole survivor of the three young girls who had light-heartedly agreed to pose for a photographer six years before. If the episode had ever occurred.

He felt in his pocket and took out the photograph of Miriam Cromer. He would need it presently for the spelling of Brodski's name on the reverse. He put it face upwards on the table in front of him. He remembered first seeing it, enlarged, in the drawing room at Park Lodge, and trying to read her character in it: an unlikely achievement. For the camera, people put on their best expressions like Sunday clothes. Hers, to be sure, was less rigid a look than photographs generally captured. That was why he had asked for a copy of this print. It conveyed something more than the stilted studio pose. But was the conflict written on her features any guide to the way she thought and behaved?

Looking at the picture now, he could not be objective. He saw it in terms of what he had learned. There were dangers, he knew, in speculating, but he saw the face of a young woman trapped. She was married to a man in love with her image. He prized her, treated and cosseted her not as his wife, but a subject for his camera. His bedroom was filled with her photographs. His adulation and excessive kindnesses only fomented her frustration, for how was she to express her resentment towards a husband who was infinitely kind?

When Perceval had added to her torment, she had found a focus for her bitterness. In murdering him, had she also been destroying her husband?

Theories. He would never know.

Truthfully, he could not tell if it was the face of a murderess.

He turned back to the report. Three girls: Miriam Kilpatrick, Judith Honeycutt and Miss C. Piper. So many names began with the letter 'C'. Constance? It did not matter any more. Finish the report.

'3. *In the second paragraph of her confession, Mrs Cromer referred to certain photographs taken in 1882 which Perceval used for the purpose of blackmail. She stated that she and two of her friends, members like herself of the*

172

Highgate Literary and Artistic Society, were induced to pose —'

It would not be Constance. Nor Charity, Cora, Clara. This was profitless. Miss C. Piper. How could he possibly know what it should be? Yet his brain continued to supply names. Mysteriously, he felt he would know if he got it right.

Cynthia, Christine, Caroline.

'. . . *unclothed or nearly so for photographs that they were informed were to be used by the distinguished artist Sir Frederick Leighton as preliminary studies for a painting of a classical subject.*'

Catherine, Celia, Charlotte.

Charlotte Piper.

It was practically right. Charlotte. *Lottie.*

Lottie Piper.

Cribb clenched his fist and beat it on the table. He knew how the name had got into his head. Millie had mentioned it that night he had woken from his nightmare and got up to make tea. The comic opera she wanted to see was *The Mascotte*, with Miss Lottie Piper.

Another blind alley. He cursed his luck. Nothing had gone right for him. Lottie Piper had no connection with the case. But the knowledge that if she had, if he had found Miriam Cromer's friend, he would have hared off to find her, was mortifying to accept. It was fate giving an extra twist to the knife. He still wanted to discover the truth.

It was too much to hope that Miriam

Cromer's friend had taken up a career on the stage as Miss Lottie Piper.

But he would try to find out.

He took down Millie's scrapbook from the shelf. Scores of pages were pasted with portraits of actors and actresses. Best to start from the back. He found Lottie Piper's picture on the second sheet, sketched in pen and ink, wide-eyed, with a skittish look, her face framed in dark curls.

MISS LOTTIE PIPER AS BETTINA IN 'THE MASCOTTE'

One of the successes of the season is that of Miss Lottie Piper in the leading role of 'The Mascotte', the Opera Comique at the Haymarket. This charming actress, the daughter of a Hampstead stockbroker, has graced several productions at provincial theatres and now reveals a talent for comic opera which is delighting audiences in the capital.

Finding a cab in Bermondsey was a tall order, but within minutes Cribb had stopped a four-wheeler.

'The Haymarket. *The Mascotte* is still running, is it?'

'Bless you, sir, that'll run for months yet.'

So he was at the stage door when her carriage drew up. She got down in a flurry of swansdown and scent, the curls proclaiming who she was, but prettier by far than the artist had made her, in a primrose-coloured skirt, emerald green jacket and matching hat with two black feathers.

'Gentlemen,' she announced (Cribb was one of five), 'how kind of you to come! I am overwhelmed, but I must tell you that I never go for supper after the performance. It's such a dreadful bore, but I find I need my sleep.'

She had blown a kiss and was through the door before Cribb or the others could put in a word. With fine theatrical timing the doorkeeper appeared from nowhere and stood with arms folded.

Cribb could have shown his identification. Instead, he started the dispersal by strolling up to Piccadilly Circus. In ten minutes he was back. There was no one left outside. Whistling, he walked in and up the stairs. He was not challenged.

He followed the scent of freesias. Her name was on the door. *Miss Lottie Piper*. Much more *chic* than Charlotte.

He expected a dresser to answer his knock. He was wrong. She came herself, opening the door just enough to look out. The penetrating stare she gave showed she was capable of dealing with callers.

'Not what you think, miss,' said Cribb. 'Police, in fact.' He took out his photograph of Miriam. Now he would know if his luck had changed. 'If you have been reading the papers . . .'

The challenge in her face was supplanted by a frown. 'Do you want to talk to me about her?' She studied Cribb's face as if making up her mind.

'I carry a card,' Cribb said, feeling in his pocket.

'Darling, I can see you're not carrying champagne,' she said.

She stepped back and let him in.

Lottie Piper thrust flowers into his arms. 'Hold these while I fill some vases. They must have been lying here for hours. I hate to see things die, don't you?'

There were three sets of mirrors in the dressing-room. Clutching the bunches of roses and carnations he looked outlandish from every angle.

'Now.' Having attended to the flowers, Lottie Piper removed her hat and arranged herself on the chesterfield, gesturing to Cribb to use a tub-chair. 'I expect my maid by half past four. May we finish by then?'

'I hope so, miss. You did recognise the photograph, then?'

She nodded. 'But I don't recognise *you*,' she said sharply. 'You must have a number, or something.'

'Sorry, miss.' Cribb reddened. 'Detective Sergeant Cribb.'

'Really? I wouldn't have thought there was much call for detection, considering Miriam's confession was in all the newspapers.'

'Yes, miss.' Cribb needed to secure co-operation here. Lottie Piper was used to speaking the best lines. 'She is due to hang on Monday. Representations have been made to the Home

Office on her behalf and it's my job to see if they hold water.'

'Has madam decided she would like to change her plea?'

Cribb was unprepared for the venom in the remark. He said tersely, 'I'll ask the questions, miss.'

She giggled nervously and tossed her curls. For a second the star of *The Mascotte* became Miss Charlotte Piper of Hampstead. 'As you wish.'

'You saw the confession in the papers. A section of it refers to you, though not by name. Am I right?'

She gave him a long look. 'Let's not be coy, Sergeant. You may ask me if I took off my clothes for a photograph. You won't make me blush, after two years in the theatre.'

Cribb was not so confident of keeping down his colour. 'What you got up to, miss, is of, er – '

'No interest? Darling, that is not gallant, even if it may be true. Have you seen any of these deplorable photographs?'

Cribb admitted he had not.

'I'm not in the least surprised,' she commented, well in control again. 'They are the talk of London and nobody has seen them.' She smiled archly. 'That three respectable young ladies should so far forget themselves as to pose for pictures of that sort!'

Cribb fingered his side-whiskers, trying to seem unconcerned. He would not admit to

Lottie Piper that he had not made up his mind whether the whole story was moonshine.

'Do you know my difficulty?' she went on. 'The stage must have corrupted me dreadfully, because the pictures I remember were absurdly tame. I admit they were not the kind of thing you would hand round at Sunday school, but I can't imagine they set Holywell Street on fire either. Five minutes from here you can see far worse without paying a halfpenny – at the National Gallery. I am obviously beyond redemption. Dear Miriam took a much more serious stand on the matter, actually poisoning a man on account of it.' The smile returned.

Cribb lifted an eyebrow. 'Do you believe that?' Before she answered, he said, 'When did you first know Miriam Cromer, miss?'

'Years ago, as small girls,' she said. 'My father met hers in some connection and suggested as she was my age that she should come to the house to play. I should think we were not more than ten years old. We had a huge garden on Hampstead Hill and Papa always said it was no garden without the sound of children playing there, so I was presented with sundry playmates, most of whom I loathed. To be fair, Miriam was easier to tolerate than most. With her fair, straight hair she was unlike me in looks, so there were no invidious comparisons. She tended to look up to me as the rightful occupant of the garden. I think she was conscious of the fact that her people were in trade, even though her father had been mayor, whereas Papa was on the Stock Exchange. Status was very important to Miriam. When I was feeling generous I would play lady's maid to her, and she was never happier. I don't pretend we were twin souls. There were times when we were not on speaking terms, and it was usually a relief when the holidays ended and I went back to boarding school, but all in all we put up with each other. As we grew older, we met less, except for church and occasional parties and *soirées*.'

'You joined the Literary and Artistic Society,' put in Cribb.

Lottie Piper smiled. 'We were Girls of the Period by then – or supposed we were. Life in Hampstead was very confining, you may imagine. Schooldays were over, and the social life revolved around St John's. We met the same people over and over. When we read in the *Express* that this new society was being formed in Highgate, we made our fathers' lives a misery until they agreed to let us join. We knew nothing about literature or art, but we convinced ourselves that people who did would find us enchanting. There was another girl we knew in the parish – Judith Honeycutt. Her father kept the umbrella shop, which was a little infra dig, but Judith was a kindred spirit, so the three of us joined together.'

'That would be 1882, would it?'

'Darling, I have no idea. I don't have a head for dates. All I remember is that the lectures were a dreadful bore, but the company was a revelation. The place swarmed with velvet coats and feather boas – another world! For half an hour or so at the end there was coffee and home-made cakes and everyone left their seats and mingled. It's laughable now, but to me at twenty that little hall buzzing with conversation was the Café Royal. I had never experienced anything so exotic. I am certain Miriam and Judith were no less enchanted. We would stay till the last possible minute we could without seeming too desperate to be noticed. Then we would catch the bus home and talk all the way of the exciting people we had met. After that it was just a question of wishing away the days to the next meeting.'

'How did the business of the photographs arise?' Cribb asked, mindful that the dresser was expected soon.

'Exactly as Miriam described it. We must have been members for six or seven months when we had a talk from someone from the Royal Academy, on Florentine Art. Fearfully boring. Afterwards over the coffee-cups everyone said how stimulating it had been, as we were bound to, and that we couldn't wait to visit the National Gallery to see the paintings he had described, just as the previous week we had gone away vowing to read every one of Milton's poems. Nobody ever asked if we did, thank God. Well, as usual on the way home I started telling the other two of the encounters I had made, when Miriam stopped me, saying she had something unbelievably exciting to tell us. I remember being dubious, having noticed she had spent most of the coffee-time with Mrs Rousby, one of the Society's founders, an over-rouged person with a domineering manner, but

I gave way gracefully. I am bound to admit that Miriam's news was more sensational than any I could supply. Mrs Rousby had said she was delighted to hear that Miriam had enjoyed the lecture, because it showed she had an affinity for art. Painting, Mrs Rousby said, was her passion. She was a personal friend of Sir Frederick Leighton, and she happened to know that the great artist was interested in finding a number of elegantly proportioned young ladies with artistic sensibilities to pose for a vast canvas he was painting on a classical theme.' Lottie Piper gave a small shrug. 'You know the rest, of course.'

Cribb wanted to hear it from her, but he was willing to provide cues. 'It appealed to you as an adventure, and you felt safe, going together.'

She nodded. 'At the next meeting of the Society, the three of us engaged to pose. We were given an address in West Hampstead, which I questioned, since I happened to know that Sir Frederick's house was in Kensington, but Mrs Rousby explained that a preliminary study was to be made by one of the artist's assistants. Left to myself, I should not have gone, but by this time not one of us would have spoiled the adventure for the others. The following afternoon we presented ourselves in West Hampstead and learned that the assistant was not a painter at all, but a photographer.'

'May I ask,' Cribb put in quickly, 'whether he was also a member of the Society?'

'He was.'

This was no time to hesitate. 'Named Julian Ducane?'

'Yes – until the name became inconvenient. You must know about that.'

'Broadly, miss. First, would you be so kind as to tell me about the pictures he took?'

She twisted a curl round her finger. 'You are a very dogged detective. Aren't you going to spare my blushes?'

He shook his head. 'If I understood you just now, there isn't much to blush about.'

'I blush for my *naïveté*, Sergeant, not for shame. Have you met Julian?'

'He is known to me as Mr Howard Cromer, miss.'

'Of course. "Julian" was right for Hampstead, but "Howard" is assuredly Kew Green. He would know. He is extremely sensitive in matters of taste. Do not under-estimate him. He is silver-tongued, Sergeant. We three girls were on our guard when we arrived at his studio that summer afternoon. In a matter of minutes he had given us a sherry and a homily on the vital contribution photography was making to the perfection of fine art. Spell-binding names were tossed so casually into the conversation that we were convinced he was on intimate terms with them – Bill Frith, Eddy Landseer, Lawrie Alma Tadema. And, of course, Freddy Leighton. Freddy, we were told, was preparing to paint his masterpiece, a canvas ten feet high and fifteen feet in length encompassing all the principal figures of Greek mythology. Some thirty gods, goddesses and nymphs were to be depicted, and Julian had been asked to take a series of photographs as preliminary studies. He showed us a selection he had already taken, and we were reassured to see that the models were without exception decently robed. In short, Sergeant, we consented to pose. The pictures he took that afternoon were unexceptionable and Julian's behaviour was exemplary. We put up our hair in the Greek fashion and wrapped ourselves in linen sheets for three or four short poses and got half a sovereign apiece for our pains. It needed little persuasion to induce us to return the following week. Do I need to go into that?'

Cribb lifted his shoulders slightly. 'You were given an extra glass or two of sherry, I imagine, and told that Sir Frederick was delighted by the previous week's results.'

'Enraptured was the word,' said Lottie. 'So enraptured, in fact, that he had asked if we would model not as anonymous nymphs, but principals. I was to be Sappho, Judith was Helen and Miriam Aphrodite. In each case, our costume amounted to a strip of muslin and a comb. The postures, I repeat, were not offensive. As Julian very reasonably pointed out at the time, how could you possibly depict a Greek goddess in stays? We got a guinea each and giggled all the way home. Quite soon, I had forgotten about it. I remember mixed feelings of disappointment and relief when the picture was not listed in next summer's Royal Academy show, but it had not crossed my mind that the photographs had been put to any other purpose.

That is really all I am able to tell you, darling.'

'There is another matter,' said Cribb as casually as he could. 'Your friend Judith died in tragic circumstances two years after this incident. You appeared as a witness at the inquest.'

Her manner changed abruptly. There was ice in her voice as she said, 'If you know about that, then you know what I told the coroner. There is nothing more to be said.'

'Touching on Miss Honeycutt's death? Oh, I'm sure you told the coroner all you were obliged to, miss.' Cribb looked down at the hat on his knees and rotated it half a turn. 'But the coroner would not have asked you the things I need to know, such as how Miss Honeycutt came to be in Ducane's employment at the time of her death.' He looked up quickly. 'You can tell me, Lottie.'

She gave him a guarded look that made him regret the impulse to use her name. 'This is a free country. She went to work for him.'

'Come now, that's no help,' said Cribb without changing his voice a semitone. 'Judith is dead. Miriam is locked in a death-cell. You are the only one who can tell me how it was that those photographic sittings led to one girl working for the man and the other marrying him. Did he blackmail them?'

'Blackmail?' Her face rippled into laughter. 'That's delicious! Darling, I'm sure you do a marvellous job in the police, but it's a terrible mistake to account for everything in criminal terms. You evidently need a few elementary lessons in feminine psychology. For a well brought-up girl to take off her clothes, however tastefully, for the first time in the presence of one of the other sex is an experience that is frightening, but not without a measure of excitement. It can stir up unsuspected emotions. Not one of us confessed it to the others, but we were deeply interested in the impression our bodies made on Julian Ducane. When he took our photographs he was scrupulously careful to treat us with equal charm, but we knew, you see, that we should meet him again at the Society. Each one of us in her private thoughts imagined him when he developed the prints becoming intoxicated with her charms. He was almost twenty years our senior and had shown no partiality to any of us, but in our girlish imaginations he was a privileged being. At the meetings we pursued him unashamedly – with what purpose it is difficult to say, because not one of us would have been allowed to walk out with a man our parents had not met. Soon there was an obvious rivalry between us. For convention's sake we rode to and from Highgate together, but once we entered that hall we were sworn enemies. Julian, poor man, was at a loss. Well, can you imagine being hounded by three starry-eyed females scarcely out of school? He tried to solve the problem by introducing us to his friends. One was his solicitor.'

'Allingham.'

'Simon, yes. There is no doubt Simon was smitten with Miriam, but Julian was the prize she aspired to. Her self-esteem demanded it. I know, because I was similarly afflicted until

I came to my senses. We were the three graces in a modern Judgment of Paris. To win was everything. Little by little, Miriam ousted us. She is one of those enviable females who can cast a spell over men. Not one of you is capable of seeing her as she really is. It takes another woman to do that.'

'Speaking for myself, I have never met her.'

'Then she has not made a fool of you, but she would. When I understood this power she had, I saw the futility of competing with her. It was only when I relinquished the contest, so to speak, that I realised how absurd it was to be chasing Julian. He was tolerably successful in his work and dapper in his dress, but a dreadful bore really. And so old! Imagine!'

'A little over forty, I believe,' Cribb said.

'Grotesque! Well, as I mentioned, I turned my attention elsewhere. Judith, too, soon after appeared to retire from the contest. She started talking to me again, telling me about young men who had tried to flirt with her across the counter in the umbrella shop. It was her way of telling me she was no longer interested in Julian, or so I understood at the time. Judith and I confided in each other a lot; it helped to heal the wounds. She was dark-haired, like me. and vivacious. She had a sense of humour, too. We had a secret joke that Julian must have sold Miriam's photograph to Burne-Jones, whose women are so solemn and underfed. Cattish, weren't we? All this went on over many months. The meetings were fortnightly, did I tell you?

'Then one day, to my intense surprise, Judith coolly announced that she had changed her job. She had been taken on by Julian as his assistant. This on the top of a bus to Highgate on the way to a Society meeting. Miriam was speechless. If you could have seen the look in her eyes, darling! It was naughty of Judith to trot it out so casually, yet I suppose she didn't want to make an issue of it. I remember Miriam sitting through that meeting stony-faced, and when the coffee came she didn't even look in Julian's direction. He came over to make conversation and she just bit her lip and walked away. It was Simon who went after her to find out what was wrong. Julian was utterly at a loss.'

'Feminine psychology isn't his strong point, either,' said Cribb.

She smiled at that.

'So Judith had cut in on Miriam's game,' he said. 'How had she managed that?'

'By sheer resourcefulness. She used the advantage she had over Miriam and me: she was in employment. She noticed in the *Express* that Julian was advertising for an assistant. She put it to her father that it was time she learned a more creative occupation than selling umbrellas. After that it only remained to convince Julian of the advantages of employing female labour.'

'What are those – apart from things she couldn't go into?'

Lottie gave him a level look. 'As well as being his assistant, she would act as receptionist. And she would bring a woman's delicacy to the re-touching and tinting processes.'

'Smart,' said Cribb. 'You have to hand it to her. There she was, installed in the studio with all day to work her charms on Julian, while Miriam sat at home fretting.'

She shook her head. 'No, Sergeant. Give Miriam credit for more gumption than that. If Julian was taking on an assistant, he would be free to delegate much of the humdrum work making negatives, or whatever they do, and devote more time to photography. Fashionable photographers, as you know, like to put notices in their windows to proclaim the prizes they have won. Julian's business was expanding, and it was time he started entering for photographic competitions. Of course he would require a model.'

'Ah.' Cribb understood. 'While Judith was in the dark-room, Miriam and Julian would be out with a camera and a picnic basket.'

'That's it. He was always saying she was photogenic, so she offered to pose for him, all very decently, I hasten to add. His Greek art phase was a thing of the past now that he was becoming respectable. Miriam persuaded him to buy her new hats and parasols and strings of beads to assist the photography. She was triumphant – and she had the relish of knowing poor Judith would be developing the pictures. Personally, I would have poured acid on them. Miriam convinced Julian that she was his inspiration. He stopped everything he was doing whenever she visited the studio. I don't know what excuses she made at home, but she was there two or three times a week.'

Cribb listened, remembering Howard Cromer had given the impression Miriam had nòt entered his life before he came to Kew.

'You would think Judith had been eclipsed,' Lottie went on, 'but not yet. I saw her one Thursday morning in Hampstead High Street. Feeling for the poor girl, I tried to pretend I hadn't seen her, but she crossed the road and, to my amazement, her face was pink with excitement. She took me into a teashop and told me she was engaged to be married to Julian! It took my breath away. The whole thing, she said, was secret until they had bought the ring. I was the first to know, because she was bursting to tell someone how happy she was. She had not told her father yet, but she was sure he would not object. Yes, they intended to break the news to Miriam that evening. Judith was certain she would share in their joy. I told her frankly not to be so sanguine about that. Miriam would be incensed. I warned her not to make it a long engagement because I was sure Miriam was too single-minded to give up. She laughed and said she had no fear of losing Julian.'

It was the girlish talk you could hear any day of the week on buses and trains, except that this was life and death.

'She said a strange thing. Had I never noticed the way Julian looked at Miriam? It was not the way a man looked at a girl he really cared for. Julian didn't see Miriam as a person at all, but a face. A face to be photographed, not kissed. She was meant to be looked at through a camera. I said perhaps he saw all women with a photographer's eye. Judith laughed again and said she was sure he did not. She was carrying the proof.'

'His child?'

Lottie nodded.

Cribb stared at her a moment. 'You didn't tell the coroner this.'

She lowered her eyes. 'I know. It seemed kinder to say nothing. By that time, Judith was dead. I couldn't alter that. Julian was up to his ears in trouble, with the suicide in his studio and the poison not being kept in a cupboard and everything. In his evidence he said nothing about the engagement, or Judith being pregnant, and nor did I. I didn't say anthing untrue, just kept silent about what she had told me. If I had spoken up, it would not have changed the verdict, but it would have ruined Julian's reputation for ever.'

'Tell me this,' said Cribb, and there was an edge to his voice. 'How did you account to yourself for Judith's death?'

Her eyes reacted with tiny darting movements. 'Sergeant, I couldn't account for it. What I told the coroner was true. The day before she died, she had been so jubilant, not worried in the least about being pregnant. The next thing I heard was that she was dead. All I could suppose was that Julian had changed his mind, and when he told her, she took poison. A woman in that condition may be subject to erratic behaviour if she gets a sudden shock.'

'Do you still believe that?'

Lottie Piper slowly shook her head. 'Since I read in the newspapers what happened in Kew, I do not. I believe Judith was murdered.'

'By Miriam?'

'She confessed to the murder in Kew, didn't she?' Lottie searched Cribb's features for some sign that he shared her conclusion. 'Her name was not mentioned once at the inquest, but she could easily have done it. She was used to visiting the studio two or three times a week. If Julian had broken the news of the engagement to Miriam that Thursday evening, she could have gone to the house on Friday knowing he was going to be out and Judith would be alone. It would be natural for them to make tea if, as I suspect, Miriam came giving the impression she wanted to congratulate Judith. She could have created an opportunity of adding the poison to Judith's cup, and then watched her die. Yes, it's a hateful thing to say about someone you have known since you were ten years old, but what other explanation is there?'

If Cribb had one, he was not revealing it. He thanked Lottie Piper for seeing him. When he got downstairs, he called in at the box office and bought two upper circle tickets for *The Mascotte*. For the Monday performance.

Chief Inspector Jowett's thin fingers drummed the edge of his desk. His eyes roved round the walls of his office, taking in the portrait of Sir Robert Peel, the stag's head, the volumes of

Archbold, Stone and the rest, anything but Sergeant Cribb, seated opposite him.

'To have come *here*, in broad daylight,' he said for the third time.

'Not possessing a telephone-set,' said Cribb, eyeing the instrument on the desk, 'I had no option but to come in person, sir.'

'You could have left a message downstairs.'

'Requesting you to come and see me? I doubt if you would have liked that, sir, so soon after yesterday. The matter requires a decision this evening, sir.'

Jowett was too upset even to light his pipe. He unscrewed the mouthpiece and peered through it at Peel. 'By Heaven, you had better be right, Sergeant. Nothing you have told me so far has altered my opinion of the case. Miss Charlotte Piper's tittle-tattle is what I would expect from a low comedy actress.'

'The daughter of a member of the Stock Exchange, sir.'

'He has my sympathy. What is this decision, for God's sake?'

'I want permission to question Miriam Cromer, sir.'

Jowett swung round in his chair, eyes blazing. 'Damn you, Sergeant, we went into this before! It can't be done. Do you understand plain English?'

'Yes, sir.'

'I asked you for a written report on your investigations. That was all I asked for, not a rambling account of your adventures at the Haymarket. Where is that report, eh? You haven't got it, have you? Yet you have the neck to come to Scotland Yard – '

'There's something else I should tell you, sir,' said Cribb in an even tone. 'There has been a development.'

'What do you mean?'

'Howard Cromer, alias Julian Ducane, has disappeared from his home. I have reason to believe he is making for one of the Channel ports.'

'Good Lord!' A glazed look spread over Jowett's eyes. 'Why on earth should he do that?'

'No fault of mine, sir,' said Cribb. 'After my interview with Miss Piper, I took a train to Kew with the intention of putting certain questions to Cromer. I felt I had enough information to get the truth from him this time. I wanted to find out why he had concealed from me the fact that he was on close terms with Miriam Cromer before he ever came to Kew, why he had withheld vital information at the inquest on the late Judith Honeycutt and what he was doing on the morning of the day Josiah Perceval was murdered. When I got to Park Lodge I was informed by a servant that Mr Cromer was not available. I put some further questions to the maid and then effected an entry into the house. From the appearance of Mr Cromer's bedroom it was clear that he had packed a number of his clothes and personal possessions and taken them with him. This the servant confirmed under questioning. It appears that Mr Cromer left the house at about one o'clock. This morning he had visited his wife in Newgate. He returned, packed a small portmanteau and left within a few minutes without taking lunch or speaking to the servants. I obtained a description, which I have telegraphed to Dover, Newhaven, Folkestone, Holyhead, Harwich and Southampton, with instructions to detain him. There was a copy of *Bradshaw* on his bed, sir.'

Jowett had gripped his mouth and chin in his right hand and was twisting the flesh without regard to appearance.

Cribb continued, 'After that I returned to London and went to Mr Simon Allingham's chambers in Bell Yard. There was a possibility that Mr Cromer had contacted his solicitor.'

Jowett managed to nod.

'I don't know if you have met Allingham, sir. He is a forthright young man. Arrogant would not be too strong a word. I asked him whether he had seen Mr Cromer in the last twenty-four hours. He tried to evade the question by asking what right I had to inquire into Cromer's movements. He wanted to know whether a warrant had been issued. I told him there were certain questions I wished to put to Mr Cromer – '

'Yes, yes, Sergeant, I'm sure you acted properly,' broke in Jowett with a sudden shift of emphasis. 'Did he tell you anything of significance?'

'He eventually admitted he spoke to Cromer at about noon, sir.'

'And . . . ?'

'He was not prepared to disclose the subject of their conversation.'

'Deuced impertinence! We could have him on an obstruction charge.'

'I think he knows his rights, sir.'

Jowett spluttered contempt.

'When I told him Cromer had skedaddled he said he wasn't in the least surprised considering the way he had been treated by the police.'

'What?' Jowett turned from crimson to white. 'What's this – intimidation? Cribb, you haven't used violence on the man?'

Cribb gave Jowett a withering look.

'I should like to know what the devil has been going on,' said Jowett, the colour rising again.

'So should I, sir,' said Cribb with no attempt to conceal his anger. 'Things have been happening that I know nothing about. I think I have a right to be informed when another officer is sent to interrogate a witness.'

'What on earth do you mean?'

'Allingham told me a man arrived yesterday afternoon at Park Lodge and gained admission on the pretext of wanting his portrait taken. From his manner and the interest he took in the details of the crime it was damned clear to Cromer that the man was a detective. Now Cromer has taken fright and cleared off.' Cribb planted his hands on the edge of Jowett's desk and leaned over it. 'I spend a week patiently building up my case, foot-slogging round London, talking to God knows how many insignificant witnesses, all to prepare the ground for a face-to-face with Cromer, and what happens? This nincompoop' – Cribb pulled a photograph from his pocket and tossed it in front of Jowett – 'goes out to Kew and puts the fear of God in him.'

The Chief Inspector picked up the picture. 'Who gave you this?'

'Allingham. It's a print from the plate Cromer made.'

Jowett studied the portrait of James Berry. 'Sergeant, this man's face is vaguely familiar, but I cannot place him. I know nothing of this.'

Cribb knew when Jowett was speaking the truth. '*Someone* must have sent him. If it wasn't you, it must have been the Commissioner.'

Jowett's hands rose like grouse from cover. 'Wait, Sergeant. We cannot leap to conclusions. Terribly unwise. I feel quite certain that Sir Charles would not . . .' He covered his eyes and released a huge sigh. 'Well, if he did, it is not for us to question his decisions. He may be privy to knowledge that we are, er . . . It will be justified in the fullness of time, I am confident.'

The fullness of time? Cribb shook his head and drew back from Jowett's desk. Was the man totally insensitive?

'The question to be decided is how to proceed,' said Jowett, piling words on his evasion. 'If Cromer proposes to leave the country we must obtain a warrant. We shall need a charge – something to detain him.'

'What do you suggest, sir?' Cribb quietly asked.

Jowett rubbed the back of his head. 'It's not so simple when you put it like that. Sergeant, the more I look at this, the more conscious I am that we are dealing with a very resourceful criminal.'

'He could be across the Channel already.'

'Then we shall extradite.'

'On what charge, sir?' Cribb knew as well as Jowett that an extradition order was obtainable only for serious crimes.

There was an awkward silence.

'We can't charge the man with murder when his wife is already convicted of the crime,' said Jowett. 'Not unless we can prove they were jointly responsible. No, by Jove, we can't charge Cromer unless his wife is pardoned. Once the fellow gets to the Continent, he'll be clean away. What is to be done, Sergeant?'

'Is the Commissioner in his office?'

'Yes, but – '

'I want permission to question Miriam Cromer,' said Cribb for the third time.

'That solicitor is here. Him that goes red to the tips of his ears when you call him Simon.'

The prisoner stopped. For twenty minutes she had been circling the exercise yard with her bed-blanket round her shoulders. It was cool in the small quadrangle bounded by cell-blocks. The sun penetrated there for four hours a day, between eleven and three. This Saturday morning it had just begun its slow descent down the granite wall.

'He is waiting in the cell,' Bell told her.

'Alone?'

'Miss, if you please.'

'Miss,' the prisoner tonelessly repeated.

'Who else did you expect – the blooming Home Secretary? Yes, he's on his own.'

Without hurrying, she crossed the cobbles to the arched doorway leading up to the condemned cells, Bell and Hawkins following.

The young solicitor jerked to his feet as if it was the Queen. Today he was in green tweeds. Each day it was different. When he smiled, boyish creases formed at the corners of his mouth.

'Miriam.'

'No touching,' Bell cautioned.

The prisoner gave him a faint smile and guided her skirts round the table to her stool.

He remained standing while the wardresses found seats. He was a charmer, this one.

'My dear, how are you this morning?'

'Impatient for news, as usual,' she answered.

He nodded. 'And you shall have some. There has been a development. If it had not kept me so busy I should have come to tell you last night.' He paused, measuring his words. 'My dear, Howard is missing. The police want to question him.'

Bell caught her breath at the news and looked at the prisoner. She had widened her eyes a fraction, but she passed no comment.

'I reminded the officer who informed me, of course, that Howard is under no obligation to notify the police of his movements,' Allingham went on. 'From the way I was questioned, you would think he was wanted on some criminal charge. Oh, they had learned from the servants at Park Lodge that he took a portmanteau with him. Scotland Yard seems to interpret that as tantamount to fleeing from justice.'

'Are they pursuing him?'

'I understand there are men looking for him at all the ports.'

'And if they find him?'

Allingham shrugged. 'If they propose to detain him, they must charge him with something.'

Bell exchanged a glance with Hawkins. From the prisoner's composure, you would think she was indifferent to her husband's predicament.

She said a curious thing. 'Then it's nearly over, Simon.'

His face lit with encouragement. 'You have been marvellous. So brave! Yes, nearly over. No doubt they will come to pester you with more questions while they have you in this place, but you must refuse to say one word unless I am present. That is your right.'

She let out a small breath, as if his words had fortified her. A tinge of colour had come back to her cheeks. Exactly why Howard Cromer's disappearance had lifted her spirit, the wardresses did not understand. They drew conclusions from what they saw. There had been opportunity enough in two weeks locked in a cell with the prisoner eight hours a day to read signals in her voice and expression. She might be sitting upright on her stool with her hands held together, but she was elated by what the solicitor had told her. If she had got the chance she would have hugged him. Between these two there were things going on.

'Simon, which of the detectives questioned you about Howard? Was it the sharp-faced man with side-whiskers or the second one, with the beard, who pretended not to be a detective at all?'

'The first.' Allingham frowned. 'Why do you ask?'

'Oh, because I believe I have seen the second. I was not supposed to, but while I was in the exercise yard this morning I happened to look up and saw a face at a window two floors up, staring down at me. He was the man Howard photographed, I am certain – the broad, scarred face, black beard and prominent eyes. Even the butterfly collar. As soon as I caught those codfish eyes he disappeared from view. I had to smile.'

Bell darted a warning glance at Hawkins. A

word out of turn now, and either of them could be up before the governor. There were things it was forbidden under any circumstances to discuss with a condemned prisoner.

Allingham had an explanation. 'Probably he was put on to the case after your trial. He would have had no opportunity of seeing you, except in photographs. He would be better employed meeting the trains at Dover than peering out of prison windows. This entire experience has done nothing to alter my low opinion of our detective force.'

She seemed not to be listening. She was looking at her fingernails, chipped and stained by prison fatigues. 'Simon.'

He reddened. She had spoken his name with a kind of ardour.

'In here, my thoughts have been much on the past,' she said, speaking in a low, earnest tone she had not used before. It seemed to Bell that it was calculated to make the wardresses feel they should not be listening. 'I think a lot about Hampstead, and the Society. Those interminable lectures that we endured for the conversation afterwards. The picnics and the outings. That trip up the river when you wore your striped blazer. I was never so happy as then.'

The young man began to look uncomfortable. 'Nor me – capital memories,' he said tamely.

'Something we share,' she said, and paused, watching him. 'In the night, when it is difficult to sleep, I find my thoughts often turn to what might have happened in my life if things had happened differently. Those were happy times and I thought I understood why, but really I did not. Simon, I was blinkered. I knew nothing of the world. Oh, I basked in its pleasures, the joys of laughter, sunshine, pretty things. Like a child. Such thoughts as I possessed were shaped by impulse. If there were things I desired, chocolates, flowers, anything, I directed all the power at my disposal to obtaining them. And because I was pretty and surrounded by people who adored me I was never thwarted. A selfish, spoilt child.'

'Come now, that's too steep,' Allingham demurred. 'You have a sweet disposition, always did.'

He was incapable of stopping her now she had started. It was so sudden that it shocked, this baring of the soul by the woman who had consistently refused to confide a word. It seemed indecent, worse than nakedness.

'I lacked any judgment, Simon,' she said in a voice that did not expect to be challenged. 'My actions were determined by impulse alone. Why do you suppose I married Howard? I could not give you a reasoned explanation.'

'In matters of the heart —' Allingham started to murmur.

'It was a whim, like everything else in my life up to that time,' she said, and her voice became less insistent, dreamier. 'Howard was there, and I wanted him. I gave it no more thought than if I had seen a bonnet in a shop window. Oh, I don't mean that my head was not full of him.

I doted on him. To me he was charming, hand-some, urbane and his prospects were boundless. Yet what I wanted in truth was gratification. I was thinking of myself.' She sighed. 'The difference in our ages, his possessive ways, his devotion to photography above all things, I dimly recognised, but I did not consider these as reasons to hesitate. I wanted him as my hus-band and that was the end of it. The end.' Her eyes moistened. 'Nothing would deter me.'

She looked down at her hands again. Nobody spoke.

'Simon, you of all people must have noticed that Howard and I . . . that the element one takes for granted in matrimony, the coming together of man and wife – '

Allingham appealed to her, 'Spare yourself, Miriam. There is no need to . . .'

The wardresses sat in silence, pretending to hear nothing, least of all what was unsaid.

The prisoner continued speaking. 'There had to be disenchantment. Really we entered into marriage without knowing each other.' She smiled faintly. 'To Howard I was something between a child and a piece of porcelain. I needed to be guarded, humoured, cherished and photographed. He liked me best when I was silent and completely still.' She looked away, in her own thoughts. 'It was difficult for me to accept after our courtship had been so full of variety and companionship. I had imagined the parties would go on as if nothing had changed. Instead I was confined indefinitely in Park Lodge. I might as well have been *here*. I even had a gaoler until I insisted she was dismissed. Howard didn't understand why I could not bear the woman. You know him, Simon. A kinder, more solicitous man does not exist. If Howard had made me unhappy from malice I could have rebelled, but he was infinitely kind. He bought me trinkets, chocolates, little toys and hid them in places where I would come upon them unexpectedly. What could I do but persevere, try to convince myself it was not the greatest mistake of my life?'

'Miriam – '

'Please listen to me, Simon,' she said quickly. 'There is not much more. I believe even now I would be ready to face a life with Howard if he had been as honest with me as he was kind.'

'What do you mean?'

She hesitated. 'That he concealed from me the truth about Judith Honeycutt.'

Allingham's features creased into a look of bewilderment. 'But, my dear, you knew about Judith.'

She looked at him with a gaze that seemed to penetrate his words and show them to be hollow.

'There was the inquest,' he said, trying to fill the space. 'You knew about the tragedy. We all did. God knows, it was catastrophic for Howard. If he had stayed in Hampstead, it would have ruined him. I don't mean to be callous about poor Judith, rest her soul, but she did not pause to think – '

She cut through his words with a bare statement. 'Simon, I know how Judith died.'

He blinked and put his hand to his face. 'Miriam, what are you saying?'

She said with deliberation, 'He told me himself. He confessed it to me as he lay beside me in our marriage-bed' – she spoke the word with bitterness – 'at a moment when he felt constrained to reassure me that he was capable of loving a woman. What consolation I was to derive from it, I cannot imagine, because he confided to me, his wife, that he and Judith . . that he was responsible for her condition at the time of her death. Whether it was true I doubt, knowing Judith as I did, but that is of no account. Howard believed it. When she told him, it threw him into a state of panic. You know how exercised he becomes about the smallest things. Imagine this! She threatened a scandal unless he married her. To Howard, the suggestion was unthinkable. Whatever had happened between them was a furtive, foolish thing, no basis for matrimony. In his mental anguish he decided there was only one escape: to do away with her.'

Allingham said, 'Miriam, for God's sake. This can't be true!'

Her colour was high. She began speaking more rapidly, unsubdued by his protest. 'You can be frank with me. You were a true friend to Howard. You saved him, told him what to say at the inquest – '

'No, no!' Allingham agitatedly said. 'Nothing of the kind.'

'Simon, he told me the truth himself. Too late. By then I had married him. Can you imag-

205

ine how I felt being the wife of a . . .' She smothered the word with an inrush of breath. 'If there had ever been any prospect of our marriage succeeding, it ended that night he told me this.'

Allingham was white. In a voice just audible, he said, 'Miriam, I knew nothing of this. Nothing.'

'I wanted you to know.'

As words stopped between them, the sound of his breathing filled the cell. The prisoner appeared calmer, her hands resting loosely on her lap while she waited for him to absorb what she had said.

In a lower key she resumed. 'Perhaps you can understand what it does to a woman to be told such a thing. The last vestiges of those girlish dreams of mine vanished in a second. My husband was a stranger to me. He has been ever since. You are not blind, Simon. You must have seen for yourself.'

'Yes,' he answered in a whisper. 'I could not fail to notice.'

'You had seen me go wilfully into marriage with Howard. You knew it was madness, didn't you?' she said. 'You foresaw the frustrations I would visit on myself. Tell me I detected from you the suggestion that I should think again. I mean those times you glanced at me in your special way or brushed your hand against mine.'

The young man flushed with embarrassment.

'I like to think you were trying to tell me in your own way about your secret sentiments. Simon, I would not speak like this if I could avoid it. Perhaps I am deceiving myself again, but I thought – I like to believe – '

He responded. 'You are right. If I could have spoken to you . . . I knew it would make no difference.'

'Yes.' A tear slid from her eye. She let it move slowly down her cheek.

They said nothing for what seemed a long interval.

The prisoner ended it. 'Simon, if there were a chance to begin again, as we were in the Hampstead days, before I married Howard, do you think it possible that you and I – knowing all you did about the kind of person I am – '

'I can think of nothing I would rather wish for,' he gently interposed.

She smiled, and sniffed to keep back tears, bowing her head.

'It is better to forget such thoughts,' he said.

Her eyes came up slowly to meet his and fix them with a look of extraordinary intensity. 'There is a way.'

He appeared not to understand.

She said, 'If they find Howard, they will arrest him.'

'They would be obliged to pardon you before any magistrate would issue a warrant,' he said.

'Howard will be brought to trial, as I was, unless he can convince them he is innocent and they drop the charge.'

Allingham still wore a frown. 'That is true, but – '

She hesitated, watching him. 'If it . . . hap-

pened . . . that he was unable to convince
them – '

'Miriam, what are you saying?'

'That I should be free in the real meaning of
the word.'

He shook his head. 'Not that way.' His hand
went to the nape of his neck and clutched it.
'No, I could never bring myself – '

'Simon, he is guilty. Judith died in agony.
Whatever view the law might take of the present
case . . .'

Articulating each word as if it caused pain,
he said, 'I could not do that to Howard.'

'Not for my sake?' she asked, her voice rising
challengingly.

'He is your husband.'

'In name only.' She closed her eyes and said,
'Simon, you are a man!'

He sat staring at her.

Bell, no less than he, was stunned. Emotional
scenes were usual in the condemned cell. Until
today, the prisoner had been unexampled in
her self-control. Cold-blooded, she had seemed.
Whatever was going on between these two –
and it was not easy to divine – the meaning of
what the prisoner had just said could not be
plainer. Or bolder.

'Simon,' she said, 'I would not ask you to say
anything that was not true. Only to keep silent
if the moment comes.' She looked steadily into
his eyes. 'Will you do that for me?'

In a dazed voice he answered, 'I do not know
that I have your strength, Miriam.'

'You are a man!' she said again. 'For me, you will be strong.'

He continued to look at her without saying anything.

'Go now,' she told him gently.

He nodded.

The prisoner's face resumed its look of passivity, as if nothing more needed to be said.

Bell felt for the keys on her belt.

The governor cleared his throat. 'You are, em, keeping well?'

'Fit for work, sir,' James Berry answered.

'Very good. Let me see. When was it we last – '

'April, sir. Mason, the Stepney murderer.'

'So it was,' confirmed the governor with a sigh. Small talk with the hangman was a cheerless business. 'Is, em, everything in order for Monday?'

Berry confirmed that it was. 'I spent an hour in the execution shed this morning. Everything's greased, sir. The traps drop nice and clean.'

The governor nodded indulgently. Berry liked it to be known that he had checked the mechanism of the gallows. An unhappy episode in Exeter Gaol three years before, when the trap-doors had three times failed to operate, had left him sensitive to criticism. 'You have the prisoner's weight and height from the records, I am sure. Has there been an opportunity . . . ?'

'Watched her at exercise this morning, sir. I see no problem. I take it the wardresses will see that the hair is pinned up. No reason to cut it.'

'That will be attended to.'

'Thank you, sir. And I assume I may visit the prisoner on Sunday evening, according to custom?'

'If you wish. The husband will be asked to take his leave of her by seven. I suggest you choose a moment half an hour after that. There are other visitors to be fitted in – the clerk of St Sepulchre's, the chaplain and myself, but you will not take long, I imagine.'

'Fifteen minutes at most, sir. I like to give the prisoner some verses of a religious character to read, as you may recollect. *My sister, sit and think, while yet on earth some hours are left to thee; kneel to thy God, who does not from thee shrink –*'

'Yes, yes. Admirable sentiments,' said the governor. 'You were good enough to provide me with a copy on a previous occasion. Berry, I think I should explain that this woman has already fully and freely confessed her guilt. It will not be necessary, or indeed appropriate, for you to inquire whether she wishes to make any statement about her crime. That is not to say, of course, that your exhortations to intransigent prisoners on previous occasions are unappreciated.'

'Only two in my experience have gone without confessing,' Berry remarked with a trace of pride.

'Quite. And concerning the arrangements for Monday . . . ?'

'I should like breakfast at half past six, sir.

My usual, if it can be arranged. I shall be in the shed until I hear the bell begin to toll at a quarter to eight. Then I shall walk up the passage and wait with the other parties who will form the procession. Punctually at three minutes to the hour I shall enter the cell and pinion the prisoner's arms. From what I am told she is unlikely to resist.'

'There will be seven male warders in attendance in case of difficulties,' said the governor. 'Two females will escort the prisoner in the procession, but at the scaffold steps they will step aside and allow two men to support her while you fasten the cap and the leg-strap.'

Berry gave a nod. 'May I inquire who else will be present, sir?'

'The chaplain, of course, the Under Sheriff and his two wandbearers, the surgeon and his assistant and two gentlemen from the press, making seventeen persons in all, apart from ourselves and the prisoner.'

'Very good, sir. Just as long as they step out, I'll have the job done as St Sepulchre's strikes the hour.'

A four-wheeler drawn by a large grey threaded through the Strand in the direction of Ludgate Hill, its destination Newgate Prison. Chief Inspector Jowett, seated opposite Sergeant Cribb inside, had the strained look of a man who had slept fitfully, if at all. The evening before, he had seen the Commissioner to request an interview with Mrs Cromer in the condemned cell. Cribb had waited in the corridor outside, in case he was called in. He was not. After forty minutes Jowett had emerged looking ashen. His lips had been moving as if he was talking to himself. Ignoring Cribb, he had returned to his office and closed the door. Twenty minutes later a clerk had come out of Jowett's office and told Cribb that the meeting in Newgate would take place next morning. Cribb was to report to the Yard at half past nine.

This morning Jowett was no more communicative. He had signalled Cribb's arrival with no more than a grunt, then picked up his hat and walking-stick and headed for the street. It was Cribb who had told the cabman where to take them.

Cribb did not need telling what had passed between Jowett and the Commissioner. The suggestion that Howard Cromer could be the real murderer of Josiah Perceval would not have been well received. Jowett had gone to the Commissioner convinced that Cromer should be arrested. Far from praising Jowett's detective work, Sir Charles Warren must have erupted. That peppery old campaigner must have seen the consequences bearing down like the Dervishes in full cry: the need to inform the Home Office that the woman was innocent; the law made a laughing-stock; the Queen obliged to sign a Royal Pardon with unseemly haste; questions in the House; cries of police ineptitude; calls for a resignation.

But he could not prevent them now from

talking to Miriam Cromer. She alone could confirm what had really happened.

Cribb had got what he wanted.

Privately still some way short of an explanation of the murder, he had seen the necessity of convincing Jowett that Howard Cromer's disappearance was as good as an admission of guilt. A hesitant Jowett would not have survived two minutes with Warren.

From the start, Cribb had known he would need to talk to Miriam Cromer himself. He needed to form an opinion of his own. Other people's assessments had supplied only contradictions. *'If you ask me what sets her apart from other women, it's an absence of pity.' 'She, poor innocent, suffered alone.' 'She is one of those enviable females who can cast a spell over men. Not one of you is capable of seeing her as she really is.'* He had not been helped by them. They presented postures, like the photographs round the sitting room at Park Lodge.

Understand the woman, see her, hear her, and he would get to the truth. He would discover why she had confessed.

His thoughts returned to the starting-point of this inquiry: the picture showing Howard Cromer at Brighton wearing the key to the poison cabinet on his chain. Its purpose was plain: to raise a serious doubt about the confession. The question nobody had asked was who had sent it. Who of the people connected with the case could have realised the significance of the picture? Miriam herself? She was in prison, and could not have sent it. Howard?

If he had sent it, he was deliberately implicating himself in the murder. Allingham? What motive could their solicitor and confidant have had for sending it?

Howard Cromer or Simon Allingham?

If Cromer had sent it in a fit of conscience, why had he waited till now to flee from justice?

His thoughts were interrupted by Jowett, who had recovered the power of speech. 'Where are we?'

Cribb looked out. 'The Old Bailey is coming up, sir.'

'Sergeant, I have decided to entrust the interrogation of Mrs Cromer to you. Your acquaintance with the more trivial details of the case is necessarily fresher than mine. I shall be present and you may defer to me on matters of procedure, but I fancy this will resolve itself quite easily now that we know the truth.'

'As you say, sir.'

The two detectives and the governor of Newgate walked stiffly through a low-roofed passage, the antipathy between them unconcealed.

'I may say that this is unprecedented in my experience,' Jowett remarked. 'I have never spoken to a prisoner under sentence of death. Tell me, Governor, what is her state of mind? How is she bearing up?'

'No better for this infliction, I assure you,' the governor answered, signalling to a turnkey to unlock the oak door to the condemned wing. 'My estimation when I saw her yesterday was that she was beginning to reconcile herself to her sentence. There was reason to hope she would face the end with dignity. God knows how this will leave her.'

'Permit me to assure you that we have no intention of inflicting distress,' said Jowett in a shocked tone. 'Our purpose is to establish the truth. We should not be here if it were not in question. I venture to suggest that you would not wish to be a party to the execution of an innocent woman.'

'She pleaded guilty and she was sentenced according to the law,' said the governor flatly. 'That should be the end of it. If prisoners understood that there was no possibility of a reprieve, our work in Newgate would be distinctly less onerous. This kind of intrusion can only undermine the authority of the law and those of us entrusted to carry it out.'

They were met by the wardress-in-charge, whose curtsey was an odd refinement in the setting. 'The prisoner's solicitor has gone in as you instructed, sir,' she told the governor. 'Begging your pardon, we found it impossible to fit chairs for all you gentlemen into the cell.'

'No matter, Miss Stones,' said the governor. 'We do not expect to take long over this.'

The cell door stood open. The governor went in first, Jowett following. Cribb waited in the doorway while the others found positions against the wall. Two wardresses and Allingham were already inside, behind Miriam Cromer, who was the only one seated, watching the influx with interested eyes.

Cribb's first impression was that she was

smaller than her portrait had suggested. But by no means was she diminished in spirit. In the graceless prison clothes, white mob-cap tied under the chin, coarse blue jacket and skirt, she succeeded still in looking elegant. She was pale from ten weeks' imprisonment, practically as colourless as the picture in Cribb's pocket. Her skin had the pellucid look of wax, and she was quite still, except for her eyes. They glinted with something between curiosity and challenge. They were confident, undismayed and, to Cribb, disturbing.

The governor announced who they were without putting it in so social a form as an introduction. 'And this is Mr Allingham, the prisoner's solicitor,' he added for their benefit.

Allingham glanced over some papers he was studying and gave the measured nod of a legal man. Here in his black pinstripe and stiff collar he would not care to be reminded of those pictures of picnics when his hand had stolen round his client's waist.

'Would you begin, Chief Inspector?' said the governor.

Jowett cleared his throat. 'My, er, assistant, Sergeant Cribb, is to put the questions.'

'Then he had better take the stool.'

Cribb edged between them and sat opposite Miriam Cromer. It was like entering a prize-ring. The situation was inimical to his style of questioning. He liked to find a common footing with those he interviewed, put them at their ease. Small chance of that in this grim place surrounded by officials.

He tried to hold her gaze in a way that excluded everyone else. 'You haven't met me before, ma'am. I took no part in the original inquiry. I was brought in to take a look at the confession you made. There are certain small matters, details really, that have come to light since your conviction. We can't square them with your account of things. No-one says you got it wrong. The mistake may be on our side. Must be.' He chanced a smile. 'Well, you're not likely to have got it wrong, seeing that you admitted to the crime.'

Her eyes focused steadily on his, conveying nothing.

'It's a fair assumption,' Cribb went on, compelled to provide his own comment. Already he could see this developing into a monologue. 'Where would be the sense in twisting facts when you know you'll end up in this place?' The question was rhetorical, but he paused before saying, 'I'd like to talk about that confession, if you don't mind.'

'I have a copy here,' Allingham announced. He leaned forward and put it into her hand. She took it without turning to look at him.

'I'm obliged to you,' said Cribb, taking out his own copy from his pocket. 'Ma'am, I want to ask you if you stand by everything you said in this document.'

She shaped her lips to answer, but Allingham spoke first. 'Naturally she does. This is an affidavit sworn before a magistrate. I must caution you not to impute perjury to my client, Sergeant.'

Cribb did not shift his eyes from Miriam Cromer's. 'May I take it that you are prepared to answer questions, ma'am?'

She nodded.

He went on, 'I want to make it plain that I'm not here to trap you. What would be the point of that? I don't go in for trickery.'

She surprised him by saying, 'You leave that to the other man.'

'The other man?' Cribb shook his head, uncertain of her meaning.

In a level voice she explained, 'The one who pretends he is not a policeman at all. The bearded man with a scar. He was sent to interview my husband on the pretext of having his photograph taken.'

'Ah. I heard about this person from Mr Allingham,' said Cribb. 'Believe me, I know nothing about him. He is not a police officer, whoever he is.'

She twitched her lips into something like a smile. 'I don't expect you to admit his existence. You wouldn't, would you? If he is not a policeman how is it that I am practically certain I saw the same man watching me from a window while I was exercising here? Is it common practice to allow members of the public into Newgate to spy on condemned prisoners, or has this place unhinged my mind?'

Whatever had been going on, it made Cribb's task infinitely harder. He turned to the governor, who reddened and gave a quick shrug.

Allingham said, 'Unless this is of any consequence, I suggest we confine ourselves to the affidavit, as the officer proposed.'

She set her mouth in a sullen little line. 'As you wish.'

Cribb resumed. This would achieve nothing unless he could win her confidence. He decided to gamble. He would let her know that suspicion had shifted away from her. 'I'll come to the point, ma'am. Shortly after your conviction, a communication from some unknown person was received at the Home Office. It was a scrap of paper cut from a photographic journal, a picture of your husband taken in Brighton on the day Josiah Perceval was killed. An arrow had been drawn on it in red ink. The arrow was pointing to the key Mr Cromer was wearing on his watch-chain. Inquiries established that it was one of the keys to the poison cabinet. The other was found on the body of the deceased. There's our first problem : how could you have opened the cabinet if one key was with your husband in Brighton and the other in the pocket of the man you claimed to have murdered?' He paused.

It was put more as a statement than a question, but he was interested to see how she reacted. From the way she held her expression, eyes steady, brows tilted a fraction, he was convinced she had learned nothing new. She was studying *him*.

'My superiors asked me to investigate,' Cribb went on. 'I studied your confession. It's a very lucid statement, if I may say so. You say on page four' – he leafed through his copy – ' "*When*

Mr Perceval went out for lunch at one o'clock, I returned to the studio, unlocked the poison cabinet, found the bottle of potassium cyanide and poured about a third of the contents into the decanter of madeira. I then replaced the decanter in the chiffonier where it was kept with the others, and locked the cyanide bottle in the poison cabinet as before. Soon after, I went out . . ." One thing you omit to state' – Cribb looked up from the confession – 'is how you obtained the key.'

Allingham put a hand on Miriam Cromer's arm. 'Say nothing.' Addressing Cribb, he said, 'My client does not wish to add anything to the statement she has already volunteered.'

As if there had been no interruption, Cribb continued, 'Naturally, I was obliged to check your husband's movements on Monday, 12th March. I learned that he was not, as we had supposed, in Brighton that morning.'

Allingham cut in again. 'I think I should point out that there is nothing in the statement suggesting what time of day Mr Cromer arrived in Brighton. Indeed, it would be impossible for Mrs Cromer to supply such information.'

Cribb persisted in addressing his remarks to Miriam Cromer. 'When I spoke to your husband he seemed unwilling to specify which train he caught to Brighton. I learned that he had engaged to be there by half past two. The delivery of wine was at noon, was it not? On the face of it, he could have doctored the decanter himself before he left. I've checked *Bradshaw*. He could have left the house as late as 12.45 and still caught the fast to Brighton from Clapham Junction at 1.12.'

Allingham made a show of protest. 'That's an extraordinary suggestion, officer. If he were here –'

'He's not, sir. He left his house yesterday afternoon, carrying a case of clothes. We don't know where he is.'

'This is absurd,' said Allingham. 'You have no grounds for suggesting that Mr Cromer would have poisoned his own assistant. What possible reason could he have for doing such a thing?'

'The reason Mrs Cromer provided in her confession,' answered Cribb. 'She was being blackmailed. Her reputation, and therefore the reputation of her husband, was at stake. It's a motive that would serve for either of them.'

Cribb's eyes had not left hers. She had listened composedly, the colour rising faintly in her face and staying there. She had not registered surprise at anything so far. He had the feeling he was speaking a part she already knew by heart.

It was time to change the lines a little. 'The man who took those photographs of you and your friends was known as Julian Ducane.'

Her forehead creased.

'Is this of any relevance?' Allingham asked.

'You should know, sir,' Cribb said without looking at him. 'He was your best friend.' To Miriam Cromer he said, 'And your husband, ma'am.'

Her lips parted and she shifted on the stool. 'I'm right, am I not?'

After a second's hesitation she nodded.

'He didn't tell me,' said Cribb. 'He told me a lot when I questioned him, but he didn't admit he met you in Highgate. No, I had to find out that for myself.'

She was frowning. 'How, exactly?'

'From a photograph,' Cribb answered. 'A picnic on the Heath. You were in it, of course, and your friends, Judith and Lottie. Mr Allingham, too.'

She fingered the strings of the prison-cap.

'It puts a different construction on things, you must admit,' said Cribb. 'Mr Allingham's presence in the picture suggested a link with Mr Cromer, which I was able to confirm later. I confirmed as well that in those days Mr Cromer was known as Julian Ducane, the man who took those unfortunate photographs of you and your two friends. The pictures were taken by the man you later married. Unhappily for you they fell into the hands of Josiah Perceval. He told you he acquired them in Holywell Street. From my inquiries I suspect he mentioned that notorious place to shock you. It's more likely that he chanced upon them in some photographic dealer's where your husband had disposed of some of his old stock – but that's unimportant. The strange thing is that when Perceval produced the pictures and threatened you with blackmail, you said nothing to your husband. It was no secret, surely? You could have confided in him without shame or fear.'

She shrugged, trying to seem indifferent, but there was concern in the blue eyes.

'It's a problem,' said Cribb, as if the worry were all on his side. 'You made a number of payments to Perceval over a period of four months. You visited a pawnbroker, put your jewellery in hock. It's evident that you hadn't spoken to your husband about it. I'm bound to wonder why.'

'She made the reason perfectly clear in her affidavit,' said Allingham. 'It could serve no practical purpose except to extend the blackmail to Howard. He is highly-strung, an impulsive man –'

'I'm aware of that, sir,' Cribb said to cut him short. 'What I'm coming to, ma'am, is that it wasn't just the photographs that you believed would alarm your husband. It was the connection with West Hampstead. Something had happened there, something that caused him to shut down his studio and go to Kew with a different name.' He paused, watching her, hearing her breath quicken. 'Judith Honeycutt's death from cyanide poisoning.'

'There was an inquest,' she said at once. 'Judith committed suicide.'

Cribb waited. Her reaction now would be crucial.

She turned to look towards Allingham. Ripples of tension had formed in her cheeks.

Allingham slipped his hand on her arm, but said nothing.

'One thing was not made clear at the inquest,' said Cribb. 'The coroner was not informed that

223

Judith Honeycutt was engaged to be married to Julian Ducane.'

'What?' Allingham said in a gasp. He withdrew his hand from Miriam's arm.

'It was never official,' she said immediately, more to him than Cribb. 'There was no ring. For that matter,' she added, facing Cribb again, 'how can you know?'

'The day before Judith died, she met Miss Lottie Piper.'

'*Lottie*?' she said in amazement. 'Lottie has spoken to you?'

'Yesterday.'

Her voice changed. It took on a harder resonance. 'Lottie never liked me. She was absurdly jealous. Do you know why? Because Howard chose *me* as his model.' She emphasised it by pressing her hand to her chest. 'I was the one he wanted to photograph. He wanted me, not Lottie or Judith. Simon, tell him that is true.'

Before Allingham could speak, Cribb said, 'Judith was expecting a child.'

She looked at Cribb and said slowly, spacing her words. 'And Howard poisoned her.'

'Miriam!' Allingham barked her name.

'Why deny it now?' she demanded. 'The girl was a slut, no better than the creatures on the streets. Worse, because her price included marriage as well as money. Howard allowed himself to be trapped.'

'I suggest you say no more,' Allingham urged.

'If I don't speak now, I shall be *hanged*, Simon. God knows, I have kept silent all this time.'

'This isn't the way,' said Allingham through his teeth.

She hesitated. Cribb watched her twist her fingers into the fabric of her skirt. Whatever Allingham advised, the impulse to talk was too strong to resist.

With an effort to keep her speech slow, she said, 'No one can accuse me of disloyalty to my husband. He has condemned himself by running away. You said just now that the motive for murdering Perceval could be attributed to Howard as much as me. You were right. *His* reputation was at risk, *his* studio.' She paused, her eyes ransacking Cribb's. 'It was not the photographs of three deluded girls in their skins that caused him to panic. It was the knowledge that Perceval had traced the pictures to Hampstead. Howard lived in dread of his past being uncovered. His nightmare was that someone would discover the real circumstances of Judith's death. When I told him Perceval intended going to Hampstead to try to trace the plates of those photographs, he was seized with fright. He was certain it would raise questions that had never been asked about Judith and himself. He believed his arrest for the murder of Judith would be inevitable if he did not act. So instead of travelling to Brighton that Monday morning, he remained at Park Lodge and put poison in the decanter. My husband is the murderer of Josiah Perceval. I am innocent.' She drew back on her stool and widened her glance to take in everyone in the cell. 'Do you understand? You have condemned an innocent woman to die!'

Cribb's eyes switched to Allingham. The young solicitor was deathly pale and beads of sweat were forming on his forehead.

'Do you have anything to say, sir?'

'Say?' Allingham shook his head.

'As Mr Cromer's solicitor,' Cribb prompted him.

Miriam swung round to Allingham. 'Simon, you must tell him. Howard is guilty. You must confirm it.'

Allingham's discomfiture was written on his features. 'My dear, I cannot do that,' he told her in a low voice.

'Simon!'

He looked away.

'Simon, for me. For *us*.' She snatched at his hand. One of the wardresses moved to restrain her. 'Leave me alone!' she blurted, close to hysteria. 'Simon, won't you save me?'

Averting his eyes, Allingham said tonelessly to Cribb, 'On the morning of 12th March, Howard Cromer was with me in my chambers here in London. He came to consult me about the blackmail, which Miriam had confided to him at the weekend. He was with me from half past eleven to just before one, when he left for Victoria, to catch the train to Brighton. My clerk will confirm this.'

'No!' cried Miriam. 'It isn't true!' She turned back to Cribb. 'Don't believe him! They want me to die, both of them. They plotted this between them. Can't you understand? They made me confess so that Howard should escape. They promised I should be pardoned. They promised!'

Cribb nodded to subdue her. 'That I believe, ma'am. You expected to be pardoned.'

He looked into the pale, attentive face. It was no longer the face in the photograph. The delicate balance of probabilities had shifted. It was beautiful, but it held no mystery. It was the face of a murderess. She was guilty not of one murder, but two. And ready to kill again. She wanted Howard Cromer to hang.

Cribb saw in her eyes an implacable force: the strength of her will. It was a force that in other circumstances might have made Miriam Cromer a social crusader of her time, for it refused to recognise defeat. But events had turned it inwards. It had become an impulse to self-gratification. She had coveted marriage. She would not be thwarted. She had murdered her own friend. Marriage had brought frustration, not fulfilment. She had discovered what it was to be the object of someone else's obsession. Isolated and unloved, yet treated with devoted kindness, she had concentrated her will into playing the part of a wife. When blackmail had intervened, she had expunged it ruthlessly. The trial and sentence had provided a fresh challenge for her strength of purpose. She had come within an ace of cheating the hangman.

Oddly, he felt a measure of respect for her. He did not want this to end in an undignified scene.

'You were cleverly advised,' he told her. 'Considering the evidence against you, it's a marvel that you had us in two minds about your guilt.'

She looked at him through smouldering eyes, trying to read his face.

'You should have heeded Mr Allingham's advice,' Cribb continued. 'Said nothing, left us to draw conclusions. Mr Allingham would not have told us your husband had an alibi until you were pardoned. But you forced it from him by accusing your husband of murder. You wanted too much out of this – a pardon and your husband's conviction. A charge of murder against your husband would never stick, and Mr Allingham knows it. The purpose of the plan was to raise enough doubts to secure your release.'

'The doubts have not all been removed,' she said with iron control. 'You seem to forget that if Howard was with Simon, as he claims, then travelled straight to Brighton, I could not possibly have unlocked the poison cabinet, since I did not possess a key.'

Cribb nodded tolerantly. 'That's a puzzle that exercised me a lot, ma'am. There's only one conclusion possible, and that is that you used Josiah Perceval's key.'

With an air of mockery, she said, 'I am supposed to have asked him for it, am I? And he, a blackmailer, meekly handed me the means of his destruction? You had better improve on that.'

'That is what happened in effect,' said Cribb, 'except that it was not the poison cabinet you said you wanted to unlock. It was the chiffonier where the decanters were kept. *That* was kept locked. Your husband being out when it was time for you to attend to the wine, you *must* have borrowed Perceval's key to open it. An innocent-sounding request which he was unlikely to refuse, seeing that he was partial to madeira. Perceval's keys were on a ring. On that ring was also the key to the poison cabinet.'

'I returned the keys to him after unlocking the chiffonier,' she pointed out.

'*Without* the key to the cabinet, which you had slipped off the ring,' said Cribb. 'At lunchtime, when Perceval was out, you obtained the cyanide and put some in the decanter.'

'If that is true,' she persisted, 'how do you explain that the key of the poison cabinet was found on the key-ring in Perceval's pocket after he was dead?'

'When you returned to Park Lodge and found the doctor there and Perceval dead, you still had the key in your possession. The doctor asked to look in the cabinet. If you had simply produced the key, it would obviously have looked suspicious. You were clever enough to tell him that the keys were in Perceval's pocket. He removed them and handed them to you to open the cabinet. You held them in your palm in such a way that the loose key appeared to be attached to the ring as you turned the lock. While the doctor was examining the poison bottles, you covertly re-attached the key to the ring. The doctor himself returned the bunch to the dead man's pocket, where it was found when the police arrived.' Cribb brought his hands together. 'I don't suggest you acted as you did to incriminate your husband. At the time, you were interested only in contriving the appearance of a suicide. When that became impossible, the other plan was worked out.' He shot a glance at Allingham. 'A gamble, that was, but a calculated one. And infernally clever. There is not a single detail I can fault in that confession. It happened just as you described it, ma'am. There were things you *didn't* go into, but the law can't touch you for something you don't say. No, if the strategy had worked, and you had got your pardon, we couldn't have brought a charge of perjury later, not for one syllable of that confession. It was absolutely true.' He folded his copy and replaced it in his pocket. 'Thank you, ma'am, for hearing me out.'

Miriam Cromer for a moment stared expressionlessly at Cribb. Then she said in a low voice, 'You had better leave me, all of you.'

The governor, forgotten, touched Cribb's shoulder. By a consensus of looks it was agreed to go.

Allingham injudiciously lingered. 'Miriam – '

'Get out!' she said in a spasm of anger. 'Stay away from here!' She wrenched at her finger and flung her wedding-ring at him. 'And tell *him* to stay away. Get out, get out, get out!'

For the return to Scotland Yard, Jowett and Cribb sat in uncomfortable proximity in a hansom.

'It flies in the face of protocol,' Jowett remarked, 'but I think it might be diplomatic to go to the Commissioner's club at once to make a verbal report on this affair. He said he would stay in London for the weekend in case of developments. I can disabuse him now of the notion that Miriam Cromer is innocent.'

'Is that what he believes, sir?' Cribb mildly asked.

Jowett turned abruptly to look at him. 'That was the advice I tendered yesterday evening, after my conversation with you. He was not at all pleased to hear it. Some of the things he said were simply sulphurous.' His eyes narrowed. 'By Jove, Cribb, if I thought you sent me in to see him with intent to mislead – '

'Not at all, sir. You drew your own conclusions from the information we had at the time.'

'Hmm.' Jowett stared thoughtfully at the shoppers along the Strand. Presently he gave a slightly embarrassed cough into his hand and said, 'It is not impossible that the Commissioner may be extremely relieved by what I have to tell him. He may express an interest in meeting you.'

'Should I accompany you to his club, sir?'

'I think not,' Jowett answered at once. 'I shall give him only the briefest summary of our findings at this stage. I doubt if your name will come up. However, I shall assure Sir Charles that a full written report will follow in due course. We shall not need to hurry over that.'

No, thought Cribb. A report to the Commissioner would take at least a week of Jowett's time. It would be polished into a model of penmanship, rational and cogent. All loose ends would be excised. And with them, the name of Cribb.

'Now that we may speak freely,' Jowett said, at his most amiable, 'I should like to know your opinion of the husband in this case. The woman's guilt is established beyond doubt. Merely out of curiosity, what construction do you put on Howard Cromer's actions?'

Cribb was not deceived. Jowett was planning that report. In case charges of conspiracy were mooted, he wanted to be certain there was a case to be made.

He answered forthrightly, 'I'll give you my opinion, sir. Cromer and Allingham are guilty men, but they plotted this so cleverly that I can't see the Director of Public Prosecutions taking it up. I believe it happened like this. The murder of Josiah Perceval was Miriam Cromer's decision alone. During the weekend she had told her husband she was being black-mailed. How he took the news can only be guessed at, but his remedy was to discuss the matter with his solicitor, which he did that Monday, sacrificing his morning in Brighton. Miriam may have been dissatisfied with Howard's remedy, or she may have decided to settle the matter in her own way on an impulse – when she had Perceval's keys in her hand. She had the means of faking a suicide, and if you want the truth, I think she would have got away with it if the poison had acted as she expected. It didn't, and ultimately even Inspector Waterlow could not escape the conclusion that he had a case of murder on his hands.'

Jowett clicked his tongue. 'That's an unnecessary slur on a fellow officer, Sergeant.'

Without altering his tone, Cribb said, 'As it's unnecessary, I withdraw it, sir. Once it became a murder inquiry, and the evidence of blackmail was uncovered, Miriam Cromer needed something quite remarkable to save her from the gallows. I believe Allingham set out to provide it. He knew the case against her was so damning that she was practically certain to be convicted. But if she confessed and pleaded guilty, capitulated, as it were, she might, on the contrary, be saved. It meant, you see, that she would be convicted on her own account of what happened, not the prosecution's. This provided the opportunity of writing a confession that was true in everything it said, but left a vital piece of information unexplained.'

'The business of the key,' put in Jowett.

'Yes, Allingham must have analysed the facts of the case and seized on this as the best chance of introducing an element of doubt. No one would mention it until after the trial. If it was brought to the Home Secretary's attention, it would have to be investigated. The plan was to divert suspicion towards Howard Cromer. Circumstances made him the only alternative suspect, but circumstances had produced two bonuses: the picture in the *Photographic Journal* and the fact that Cromer was not in Brighton on the morning of the murder. The picture was sent to the Home Secretary. In due course, I was sent to see Cromer. He was evasive about his movements. He hedged about the train he caught to Brighton. They must have known we would check the minutes of the A.G.M. and discover he was absent in the morning. And they still had their trump to play.'

'Cromer's disappearance?'

Cribb nodded. 'That was calculated to force us into action. With Howard on the run like a guilty man, we would need to consider extradition. The gamble was that in order to obtain a warrant, we would have to arrange a pardon for Miriam Cromer. As soon as she was pardoned Howard would surrender to the police. He would announce that he had an alibi for the morning of the murder, and Allingham would confirm it.'

'But that would confirm his wife's guilt,' said Jowett.

Cribb had waited for this. '*Autrefois Convict.*'

'I beg your pardon.'

'Don't you have French, sir? A legal expression. It dates back to common law. A person cannot be prosecuted twice for the same offence. Even if we knew Miriam Cromer was a murderess and brought her up before a magistrate, she could plead *Autrefois Convict* and walk out a free woman.'

'I am aware of the law, Cribb,' said Jowett sourly. 'It was the terminology that escaped me.'

In case something else escaped the Chief Inspector, Cribb said, 'It was a very cunning idea, sir, not easy to unravel. But like all ideas it depended on people to carry it out. Their nerves were tested to the limit. Miriam Cromer in the death-cell waiting for Howard to make his move. Howard, who had to tread the tight-rope between supplying information and con-cealing it. Allingham, the architect of the plan, knowing either of the others could ruin it and destroy his career. Howard was the first to put a foot wrong. The unforeseen intervened, in the person of the bearded man they decided was a detective. I still don't know who he was – probably never will. I was livid when I heard about him, but on consideration I have to admit he did us a good-turn. Howard Cromer was so anxious for an indication that the police had taken his bait that he assumed this visitor was one of ours, instead of some morbidly-inclined member of the public. By inviting the man in, humouring him and taking his picture, he showed how desperate he was to interest the police in himself. And of course I heard of it from Allingham, who was no less interested to confirm whether the man was from the Yard. It was an instructive incident, and it need never have happened if Cromer had politely sent the man away. It made me think.'

'I must say, I thought it suspicious myself.'

Cribb disregarded the contribution. 'The next day Howard Cromer vanished.'

'The trump card.'

'I couldn't ignore it,' said Cribb. 'I decided to make use of it myself – to secure the meeting with Miriam Cromer. She surprised me. I didn't expect to be confronted by a woman so fully in command of herself. The only way I could see of getting at the truth was persuading her that we had swallowed the story and simply wanted evidence of Howard's guilt. I thought she might become over-confident. That, as you know, is what happened. She wasn't satisfied with the original plan. She had thought of an improvement. Instead of letting us draw our own conclusions as to Howard's guilt, she proceeded to confirm them, and she expected Allingham, out of regard for her, to withhold the alibi. Then she would be pardoned, Howard would hang and she could begin a new life with Allingham, who had always admired her. She believed she could count on Allingham's co-operation by convincing him that Howard had murdered Judith Honeycutt and so deserved to hang.'

'For another murder?' said Jowett. 'That's perverted logic, if ever I heard it.'

'Ten weeks in custody had given her time to fashion the facts to suit her purpose,' said Cribb. 'She over-reached herself. Allingham might have allowed emotion to over-rule his judgment until he heard what Lottie Piper had confided to me – that Howard had engaged to marry Judith Honeycutt. Nothing had been said at the inquest about that betrothal, nor had Allingham been told of it. He saw in a flash that Miriam had had the motive for murdering Judith: she had wanted Howard for herself.'

Jowett stared bolt-eyed at Cribb. 'She murdered the Honeycutt girl as well?'

'I'm sure of it. Proving it now would help nobody, but it's the only explanation. Consider how she behaved under the threat of blackmail. For weeks she said nothing to her husband about her ordeal. She made her own arrangements to meet Perceval's demands – and it's no light matter for a woman of her class to enter a pawnshop. Yet why didn't she take Howard into her confidence? He knew about the photographs: he was the photographer. If the danger were simply the threat of scandal to their livelihood it would have been natural for her to turn to him, but she didn't. There was a greater danger that only Miriam Cromer understood. Imagine what Howard Cromer's reaction would have been to the news that the wife he worshipped was threatened with blackmail by his assistant. He would have been outraged. To submit to a cheap threat of that sort was unthinkable. I believe he would have dismissed Perceval instantly from his employment and threatened him with prosecution. Howard, you see, could not appreciate the greater danger to his wife – that Perceval by chance had unearthed a link in the chain that led to Judith Honeycutt's murder. It was safer, Miriam Cromer decided, to make the payments herself, buy the photographs and say nothing to Howard, who still believed Judith's death was due to suicide. So that was what she did, until the fateful day when Perceval told her he was going to Hampstead to try to buy the plates. The thing she feared most was about to happen. Perceval would trace the name of Julian Ducane and very probably learn the story of Judith's death. What Miriam had thought was buried was about to be disinterred. She decided to poison Perceval as she had poisoned Judith.'

'So callous!' Jowett exclaimed. He shook his head. 'And such a fine-looking woman. A picture.'

'A picture,' Cribb repeated, thinking his own thoughts.

The cab turned left in Great Scotland Yard. 'Sergeant, I salute you!' Jowett said in a fit of generosity. 'Between us, by Jove, we have saved the law from a contemptible plot. I shall put you down here. You may be sure that everything you have told me will be conveyed to the Commissioner. In my own words. Depend upon it, I shall omit nothing of importance.'

Cribb got out of the cab, touched his hat and made his way unimportantly home.

Towards midnight, James Berry turned the latchkey and let himself into his house in Bilton Place, Bradford. He was quiet about it. Upstairs the three youngsters and his mother-in-law would be asleep.

His wife came along the passage with a candle. He put down his leather bag and kissed her. 'You're later than usual,' she said. 'Nothing went wrong?'

He shook his head.

'It were a woman, weren't it?'

'Aye.'

'She deserved to go, didn't she?'

'It were never in doubt,' said Berry.

'What kept you in London, Jim?'

'Business.' He had finished his work in Newgate by ten; it had taken almost an hour to penetrate the crowd outside Tussaud's. One of the police had told him ten thousand were massed in the Marylebone Road. 'Average in my experience,' the constable had said. 'Funny old world, isn't it, when ten thousand turn up to see one more sinner installed in the Chamber of Horrors? I know they are the actual clothes she wore in the dock, but it's still only a waxwork. That's all they've come to see – one figure in wax.' Berry had murmured, 'Two,' and modestly moved on.

'I kept some stew,' his wife said. 'I hope you're hungry.'

'Put it on table and see.' He hung his coat on the hallstand.

'Jim! That's a new suit!'

'Aye.'

'You *do* look nobby! Grand! But where's the other?'

'I left it behind.'

She frowned. 'There was some wear in it yet.'

'Ay.' He went to the mantelpiece and picked up the letters from behind the clock. 'Anything in this lot?'

'Only that large one. Postman had to knock for that. Came Saturday.'

Berry examined it, a large white envelope, too stiff to bend, his address inscribed in a fastidious hand. It was postmarked 'Kew'.

'You can open it, love,' he said.